SAYING UNCLE

GREG F. GIFUNE

D1511024

This Edition
September 2008

Published by:
Delirium Books
P.O. Box 338
North Webster, IN 46555
sales@deliriumbooks.com
www.deliriumbooks.com

ISBN 978-1-929653-99-7

For Carla, Brandon, Kendyl, and Hayley

Acknowledgements

Thank you to Jo Popek, former editor of *The Roswell Literary Review*, the magazine that originally published the short story on which this novel is based, for her encouragement and editing expertise when this was still a short story concept. Thanks also to Sandy DeLuca for her friendship and for her efforts in first getting this novel out to the public. A big thank you to Tom Piccirilli for all his support, friendship, thoughtful advice, and for taking time from his busy schedule to pen the introduction. Special thanks to Shane Staley for believing in this novel, getting it back into print and bringing a whole new group of readers to *Saying Uncle*. Finally, as always, thank you to my wife Carol for her patience, grace and love.

INTRODUCTION

TOM PICCIRILLI

The fact that you're holding this book in your hands proves that you're on the righteous path where your reading tastes are concerned. You're one of the enlightened ones, you're in the know, and you're way out front of the cripples on the slow curve to finding their way to the truly hip reading material.

You've either read Greg Gifune's work before or you've heard about him enough that you finally decided to invest. Maybe you've managed to score copies of *The Bleeding Season*, *Dominion*, *A View From the Lake* or *Deep Night*. If so, hold onto them, kids, those are precious items on your shelves.

Greg deserves to break in a big way, and for all the reasons you're about to find within the pages of

5

Saying Uncle.

Here you'll discover a highly literate, emotionally complex coming of age story fused to a returning-home-to clean-up-personal-history tale. Within that framework you've also got plenty of noir moodiness, crime elements, small town drama, and edgy family anguish.

For such a short novel, *Saying Uncle* is steeped in some serious atmosphere. It's the kind of book that you'll want to rip through and yet also savor. You'll reread passages for the pure poetry of sound as well as for the dazzling imagery. It's that lush and affecting.

Once you pick this baby up, prepare to be cold, to be chilled, to feel the freeze all around you, the snow coming down and landing on the back of your neck. It's a testament to Gifune's literary prowess that he can give you a real shiver of trepidation in the warmth and safety of your own home. I'm not trying to sell you a bill of goods – *this bad boy book right here is so terrifying it'll make you curl up in the corner trembling uncontrollably, it'll make you hawk up your heart and spit out your fucking liver!*–nah, man, let's save the hyperbole for someone who needs it. Gifune sure as hell doesn't.

The truth is, he'll get you chilly where it counts — down deep, where all the truly troublesome stuff is. He'll dredge up some of that and spoonfeed it back to you, because that's what the best writers do. They make a connection with you in the places you don't want anybody to connect with. It's the thing that gets to you, dig? The thing you forever want to tuck away and keep under lock and key, in the pit of your most fierce and fearsome memories, where you're a coward, where you let your family slide away through your fingers, where you finally come home to where they know your true name. Try as you might to keep all that locked away, Gifune still manages to crack your safe and riffle through your secrets. Your guilt, your fear, your rage, your weakest moments when you should've cut left instead of right, when you should have stood up instead of backing off.

That's what's at the core of *Saying Uncle*, and that's why it's bound to truly make you flinch.

Think I'm bullshitting you?

Well, grab your winter cotton socks and pull Grandma's crocheted blanket up around your shoulders, start a fire, and get ready to get cold and cry uncle.

—Tom Piccirilli
January 7, 2008

*"All violence, all that is dreary and repels,
is not power, but the absence of power."*

–Ralph Waldo Emerson

WINTER, 1999

"No man chooses evil because it is evil; he only mistakes it for happiness, the good he seeks."

—Mary Wollstonecraft

1

To this day I don't know why they called me.
My mother probably gave them the phone number
with the intention of delaying the inevitable and
sparing herself the horror of seeing her only brother
like that. Maybe she was still in shock and hadn't
been thinking clearly, I can't be certain. What I do
know is that identifying Uncle Paul's body for the
police that night was just as upsetting as I'd
imagined it would be. It struck me as darkly ironic
yet necessary that I should be given this task, as
without witnessing his lifeless remains firsthand the
idea that he could really be dead would have
remained beyond belief. What I pictured instead of
those remains were the search parties combing the
woods and beaches so many years before. People in
town banding together, many of them completely
unaware of whom the person they were searching
for was but knowing it was something they had to
take part in. An effort, perhaps, even by those
removed from the missing boy, from the entire situ-

ation leading up to it and the aftereffects left in its wake, to connect with some larger portion of humanity beyond their reach until then. It was a time when people in towns like ours still cared—or at least pretended to care—about the people next door or across the street, because in many ways their friends and neighbors and even the majority of those town residents they didn't know, but knew of, defined us all.

For some reason I remembered my grandmother's funeral too, and how young I was at the time; milling about the funeral parlor aimlessly while adults around me cried and spoke in rapid whispers. I remembered standing in the front pew at church hours later as they wheeled her casket down the aisle and presented it to the altar. Both were covered in white, a defiant statement of clarity in the face of darkness, or maybe because there was just as much purity in death as there was in life. I remembered a woman singing, "Here I am Lord" in a beautiful soprano that echoed through the curved walls of the small church, and how it brought up the emotion in everyone, a reminder that my grandmother had gone on to some other place where we would all one day follow.

And what I thought about most when I remembered that day, and the day years later when all those people searched so frantically for a boy gone missing, was that none of those things would ever happen for his family, for his friends and neighbors, because right or wrong he was never coming back. Not to live, not to die. He was just gone.

As the past faded in favor of the present, an over-weight, grim-faced detective greeted me at the entrance to the morgue, introduced himself with a nod and in an officious tone, thanked me for coming. Without further comment he escorted me across the foyer, past a series of darkened offices and into a labyrinth of hallways. After what seemed like an eternity we reached the room where the body was being stored.

The detective hesitated, his hand on the door. "Ready?"

"No," I said.

Whenever my phone rings in the night, I am reminded of him still.

* * *

I cannot recall a time when I was not close to Uncle Paul. My mother's only brother, he was a year older than she, and due to the absence of my father, an integral part of our lives from the beginning. My father worked in insurance sales, and although he didn't abandon us until I was five, my memories of him are vague at best. When I see him in my mind's eye he is a tall and lanky man in an inexpensive wrinkled suit, a mixed drink in one hand and a cigarette in the other. I remember being near him, sitting on the floor playing or coloring in one of my books while he sat in his chair, but I have no memory of ever having had a conversation with the man. More boarder than parent, he seldom used our home for anything other than a place to sleep.

The fact that his wife and children resided there as well seemed irrelevant to him somehow. For years I tried to remember the sound of his voice but it always alluded me, and in the end he became little more than a phantom.

My mother married too young, and by the time she was twenty she had given birth to my younger sister, Angela, and myself. Memory dictates she was a good and loving mother, but with the passage of time I have come to realize she was never a particularly happy person. Raised in a traditional Italian-American family, she was taught to be somewhat subservient to men, a second banana, as it were, to her male counterparts. In families such as ours, women often wielded significant power but behaved, at least on the surface, as if it all rested in the men's hands. Like an actor miscast, for my mother it was a role she seldom played convincingly but assumed nonetheless.

We lived in Warden, a primarily working-class town located on the southeastern coast of Massachusetts not far from Boston. It was a pleasant place to grow up, at least for a little while.

From the time my sister and I were quite young Uncle Paul became something of a surrogate father. He was young himself (only in his middle twenties when Angela and I were still in elementary school), and although he wasn't married and had no family of his own, he had a wonderfully natural way with children. He was different somehow from other adults in the sense that he seldom behaved like one, a trait that made it easier for Angela and me to relate to him. He wasn't immature, rather carefree and confident, someone who treated us and spoke to us like we were thinking human beings who deserved as much respect as anyone else, children or not. I suppose it was his air of confidence and control I envied most. As I later learned, there were many reasons for him to be full of nearly constant worry, but that was a side of him he rarely allowed us to see. He had two very divergent lives and for us existed only during those times when he was in our presence, like a toy that comes alive in the hands and mind of a child but ceases to exist once it's out of sight and the toy box lid is closed.

Looking back now I realize there were many things I should have questioned more diligently. Angela and I never knew for sure what Uncle Paul did for a living. He told us he was a businessman but never elaborated beyond that point. He seemed to work when he felt like it, as there were often lengthy periods when he was free to do as he pleased. Yet he always had money. He wasn't rich by any stretch of the imagination, but always had a stack of cash that he kept in a wad secured by a shiny billfold in the left pocket of his trousers. He usually wore tailored, double-breasted suits and calfskin loafers, but even his casual apparel was expensive and stylish. On his left hand he wore a diamond ring and an expensive watch, and strung loosely around his right wrist was a gold her-ringbone bracelet. Unlike most men in town Uncle Paul's hands bore none of the scars or patches of rough skin generally associated with years of manual labor, and I rarely recall seeing him look disheveled.

I have always believed my mother knew from the start the sorts of things her brother was involved in, but when anyone asked her answers were just as vague, and Angela and I soon learned that when it came to our uncle those types of inquiries would not be answered with any degree of specificity.

It also seemed odd to me that he was almost always alone. He seldom spoke of friends or business associates, and although at times he mentioned women, I had known him for years before I met one of his girlfriends. None of his relationships with women ever seemed terribly serious, and on those rare occasions when I met someone he was seeing, they were gone from his life as quickly as they'd entered it.

He was less than six feet tall but carried himself like a much larger man. His build was compact and powerful; his hair dark, combed straight back and secured in place with styling gel, and his features were attractive if not traditionally handsome. His complexion was light olive, and although his nose was a bit large he wore it well. When he smiled he did so with his eyes first, his thin lips slowly curling just enough to reveal a hint of teeth seconds later. I remember the rapid cadence of his speech and even the specific tone of his voice, as it had a whispery sound often found in people who smoke.

Uncle Paul, or simply "Uncle" as we called him, was the lone positive and consistent male influence in our lives. Since our father's departure we'd had no contact with the members of his family, and both our grandparents on our mother's side had died by the time I was four and Angela just a toddler. Our mother and Uncle Paul were born to older parents who met later in life. Tragically, they died when their children were still quite young and their grand-children mere babies.

After my father left, our mother dated from time to time, but those men had little interest in two young children and were generally gone before we had the chance to get to know them. Choosing men was never my mother's strong suit, though I under-stand now how difficult it must have been for her in those days. She was a single mother with bills that far exceeded her wages as a cashier at a nearby discount department store, and while she must have been miserable, her pain, fear and loneliness were well hidden from us more often than not.

Because she'd married so young and had babies while most women her age were in college, when our father left she was the sole supporter of our family and had to do the best she could with no training and only a high school education. But even when I was very young, Uncle's financial contribu-tions to our family were evident. Looking back now I realize he was probably the only reason we avoided public assistance.

Besides our father, the only serious relationship my mother had was with a man named Ed Kelleher, a local welder who eventually moved in with us for a short time. Uncle didn't approve of the arrangement, which led to several arguments between him and our mother. A loud and abrasive man, Ed Kelleher frequently took it upon himself to reprimand my sister and me without good reason. Our very existence seemed to annoy him. On one occasion he decided Angela needed to be punished for spilling a glass of milk on the kitchen floor. It had obviously been an accident, and even though he knew our mother didn't believe in raising a hand in anger against children, she'd been at work at the time, and Ed put Angela across his knee and administered a spanking. She was five at the time.

After Ed's threats, neither of us told our mother what happened, but later that evening, once I was certain my mother and Ed had gone to bed, I crept into Angela's room to check on her. Only eight myself, when I saw her eyes fill with tears a rage exploded through me the likes I had never felt before. I sat on the edge of her bed, gently rubbed her back and whispered my assurances that everything would be all right. Her pain and tears seemed ghoulishly out of place in her bedroom, a space filled with stuffed animals and storybooks and dolls.

"We should tell Mom," I said.

In a tiny voice she said, "Ed said not to or he'd hurt her too."

"Everything's going to be all right." I told her I loved her and kept rubbing her back until she finally drifted off to sleep a few moments later.

And then I called Uncle.

He arrived early the next morning. I was playing in the front yard when his black Camaro pulled in, tires crunching gravel in the driveway. It was late

July and the humidity was already rising, but when he stepped from the car he was wearing a charcoal gray suit and a pair of mirrored sunglasses. By the time he'd crossed our small yard his jacket had been removed.

"Do me a favor and hold this for me a minute," he said.

I wiped dirt from my hands and took the jacket as he'd taught me, gently, and by the collar. "Ed spanked Angela."

"You already told me that." With methodical precision, Uncle neatly rolled up his sleeves. "I'll handle it. Where's your mother?"

"In the kitchen. Ed's upstairs sleeping."

"And Angela?"

"She's in her room."

Uncle gave a quick nod, removed his sunglasses and handed them to me. "Don't get your fingerprints on the lenses, all right?"

Standing there with his sunglasses in one hand and his jacket in the other, I watched him go inside. After a moment my mother emerged from the house with Angela and sat with her on the steps, staring at me.

"Where's Uncle?" I asked.

"He's having a talk with Ed," she answered flatly. "That's what you wanted, wasn't it?"

Before I could respond the screen door swung open and Uncle sauntered out. He glanced at my mother, his face showing no emotion whatsoever. "You better call an ambulance. Ed fell down the stairs."

As my mother stormed into the house Uncle signaled me to bring him his things. Once he had them back in place he pulled some cash from his pocket, peeled off two fifty-dollar bills and handed them to me. "Give this to your mother once she calms down. Tell her to go get some groceries."

"Thanks, Uncle."

"Thanks, Uncle," Angela echoed.

He leaned over and kissed the top of her head, then looked back at me. "Soon as he gets back from the hospital Ed's moving out. Your mother's pissed but once she calms down a little make sure you tell her what he did to Angela, and what he said he'd do if she told. She'll still be mad for a while but she'll understand and she'll get over it."

My mother didn't speak to me for a few hours, but Uncle was right, it didn't last. Later, when we talked about it, I learned she was glad we had told someone, but would have preferred it be she rather than Uncle.

"He loves us," she told me, "but you know how he can get sometimes."

I certainly did. Regardless, my mother never let another man live with us again. At the time, with the purely selfish motivations children often have, I never stopped to think about what that meant to her, what sort of sacrifice it meant in her life to never be able to enter into a serious relationship with a man without feeling she was somehow exposing her children to something they were better kept away from. Our unassuming little house became something of the sanctuary Angela and I had wanted it to be previously, a place where we were safely tucked away from the rest of the world and all its potential horrors. Our mother was all ours, concealed in a cocoon we thought would never again be broken, but that had begun to slowly suffocate the life from her even before the whole thing came crashing down.

Though the episode with Ed Kelleher will forever stand out, most of my memories of Uncle to that point are equally poignant but far less dramatic. I remember him sitting with Angela on the floor of her bedroom, playing with dolls and plastic tea sets. I remember him coming to visit on Saturday mornings to watch cartoons; the sound of his laughter and suspecting he was having even more fun than we were. I remember him teaching me how to play basketball and how he'd usually let me win. I remember him coming to see our school plays and recitals, clapping and cheering louder than anyone else, and chaperoning each year on father-son field trips. I remember countless visits to the nearby zoo, having lunch at our favorite restaurant and concluding the day with a trip to the local toy store where Angela and I were allowed one item of our choice, regardless of price. I remember him helping me with homework and marveling at how intelligent he was despite his lack of formal education, and how he gave me pointers on defending myself after a bully at school smashed my brand new Charlie Brown lunchbox over my head. I remember him clowning with my mother—snatching her up when a particular song came on the radio and how they would dance around the kitchen holding each other and laughing while Angela and I gleefully looked on, thrilled to see that rare instance when our mother seemed genuinely happy to be alive.

Of course I idolized my uncle, so a good portion of my remaining childhood was spent trying to please him and earn his approval.

"The difference between a boy and a man is that when a man gets knocked down he always gets up," he used to say. "That's what life is, Andy, getting knocked down and learning how to get back on your feet. There's no shame in going down, but never *stay* down. Get off your ass and fight back. It's not easy being a man, but what choice have we got?"

No truer words were ever spoken.

I was fifteen when everything changed forever. The events that summer helped shape me as a human being and define me as an adult, but also tore a wound through the heart of our family that would never completely heal. For any of us.

2

The room was cold, sterile and antiseptic smelling.

On shaky legs I moved closer to the coroner's slab and gazed down into Uncle's sightless eyes. Shocked to find them open, they were fixed in a blank stare and covered with an odd film. A white towel had been draped over the top and front of his head in an apparent effort to spare me from seeing the trauma his skull had sustained.

He was much older than I remembered him, his skin looser and the lines in his face more pronounced. The hair close to his temples was streaked with gray, as was the stubble along his chin and neck. He apparently hadn't shaved the day he'd died, and that struck me as wholly unlike him. At least the version of him I had known.

Then again, I thought, hair continues to grow after death, so maybe it was—

"You all right?"

"Yeah." I turned away from Uncle and returned

my attention to the dour-faced detective. "That's him."

The detective nodded and a man in a white lab coat I had forgotten was there slid the body back into the wall unit. "I realize this is a difficult situation," the detective said, "but I need your signature on a few documents and then I'll let you get out of here."

We stepped back into the dimly lit corridor. "Can you tell me what happened?"

"The case is still under investigation so I'm not at liberty to go into any specifics at this time." He hesitated, allowing the awkward silence to take hold. "But I can give you the basics."

Visions of Uncle's death mask flashed through my mind. "I just saw the basics."

* * *

My wife once described me as a helium-filled balloon floating along the landscape, occasionally dropping low enough to scrape the Earth but always returning to the air before a fixed location could be established. It was her way of telling me I behaved more like a spectator to life than an actual participant in it, and I suppose in hindsight she was right. It was a role I assumed from a very young age, though in the summer of 1979, at fifteen, I did not yet know why.

But for Desmond Boone, my sidekick since we were in the first grade, I had few friends, was not good at socializing and spent most of my free time pounding away on a portable typewriter Uncle had given me for my thirteenth birthday. While most children my age spent the summer months at the public beach or playing sports, I could either be found killing time with Desmond, who always went by simply: *Boone*, or huddled at the picnic table in our backyard writing stories. Even though I didn't know why I wanted to be a writer, like a ratty old jacket, it just seemed to fit, and I pursued it frantically, writing nearly every day, sometimes for hours at a time. Boone loved my stories and was the only person on the planet convinced I'd one day be a famous author.

But then poor Boone—as loyal and dedicated a friend as he was—believed in a lot of foolish things, me among them, I suppose. He came from a dysfunctional home and was verbally abused by his alcoholic father, who took particular glee in pointing out what a devastating disappointment Boone was and how he would never measure up to his older brother Jonathan, a star athlete without a quarter of the intelligence Boone possessed, but who could throw a ball well and was thus rather ironically treated like a higher life form.

I had always been a decent athlete myself, but never took it all that seriously. Where I was quiet and more introverted, Boone used humor for defense and food for comfort. I kept mostly to myself, and he cracked jokes and drew attention. I was thin and wiry; he was quite chubby. Boone was large for his age, a big-boned kid with a shock of unruly reddish brown hair, striking blue eyes and a pudgy face sprinkled with freckles. I was a bit small for my age, with dark hair and eyes and a rather brooding guise. We offset each other nicely. Like me, he was ignored more often than not by most everyone else, and in each other we saw certain traits lacking in ourselves, which is perhaps why we got along so well, and over time became the best of friends.

In the summer months Boone and I earned spending money by mowing and raking several yards in the neighborhood. We'd get to work early so we could be finished by noon, before the humidity became too unbearable, and so we'd have time to spend a bit of our earnings on cheeseburgers and frappes at Mickey's, a diner downtown, and plan the remainder of the day.

Generally we'd hit the drugstore first, then make a beeline for the book and magazine section at the rear of the store so Boone could grab the latest comic books and I could check the paperback novel rack. That summer I had become hooked on Alistair MacLean adventure novels, and bought and read one nearly every week. Boone was a Captain America fanatic and hadn't missed an issue in years. Mission completed at the drugstore, we'd ride our bikes to the beach, take a quick swim then head back to my house.

Eventually, after playing some records or talking for a bit, I'd find myself sitting at the picnic table with my typewriter, working away on a new story while Boone sat quietly across from me reading his comic books and awaiting my next tale.

It is that memory I recall most fondly when I think of Desmond Boone. The times we spent together at that picnic table, beneath a summer sun, content to simply be in each other's company.

The day before it all started, Boone and I had finished our lawns, collected our pay and made our usual rounds to the diner and drugstore, and were on our way back to his house so he could put away his newest comic book. He kept them all meticulously stacked and organized in a series of cardboard boxes under his bed, and since on this day the issue he had purchased was a special edition, Boone was adamant about getting it safely tucked away in his room before anything happened to it.

Boone lived a few streets over from my own, but in our neighborhood all the houses looked pretty much the same: rows of small, modest homes with tiny front yards and slightly larger backyards. It was a lower income, working-class area, where most people rented rather than owned. I suppose Boone, like us, was poor, but we didn't realize it at the time. Things just were the way they were, and since we'd never known anything else, it didn't occur to us that *we* were the "poor" people folks on the other side of town often referred to.

To us, people like Beau and Lonnie Miller were poor. They lived with their mother in a literal shack on the edge of town, adjacent to the state forest, and were the resident whipping posts when it came to such discussions. No matter how bad off anyone was, they always looked to the Millers and labeled them as worse off, thereby perversely elevating themselves, if only in their own minds. I never knew Beau and Lonnie that well because they were a couple years older than I was and ahead of me in school. But I often saw them around town or congregated in their yard working on some archaic mini-bike, and always wondered why it was considered universally acceptable in town, regardless of neighborhood, to make sweeping, unfair and often outright cruel assumptions about people who had done nothing to deserve such treatment. Apparently their crime was poverty, and in crossing that line from poor to impoverished, it had somehow been determined that a perpetual open season on their dignity was not only tolerable, but encouraged.

Whenever I heard someone make a joke or ridicule them, I always found myself curious as to whether that was how the people across town talked about me. It all struck me as foolish even then, monumentally unimportant in the overall scheme of things, since everyone, it seemed, was just trying to get through life as best they could. And one of the life lessons I learned that summer was that no one escapes unscathed. No one.

As Boone and I crossed the sidewalk and approached his house, Boone's father emerged from the front door to greet us, hands on his hips. His hair was mussed and he was unshaven and wearing a bathrobe despite the fact that it was early afternoon. We hesitated just inside the property line and I felt the usual discomfort well up at the sight of him. He squinted, shielded his eyes from the sun with the back of his hand and peered down at his son. "What are you doing, boy?"

"Hi, Dad."

"Hi, Mr. Boone," I added quickly.

He stood there silently a moment then dropped his eyes across Boone's body. Due to the heat, we had removed our shirts and tucked them into the back of our shorts. "Jesus H. Christ," he said through a heavy sigh, "will you take a look at this one."

The slurred speech and overwhelming stink of liquor signaled that as usual Boone's father was drunk.

"Do the neighborhood a favor and put your shirt back on, boy. Christ almighty, you got bigger tits than your mother."

Boone turned a bright red color that began in his cheeks and spread throughout his body like a recently injected dye. He fumbled for his shirt and quickly slipped it back on. "I just came to drop this off," he said quietly, holding up his comic book, "then me and Andy are going back to his house."

His father glanced at the comic book and chuckled. It was a mean laugh, void of joy. "Fifteen years old and still reading the goddamn funnies."

"They're comics, Dad."

"Big fat slob walking around with funny books at your age—Jesus—like some kind of faggot. What the hell is wrong with you, boy? *What* is your problem?"

I tapped Boone's arm and motioned for us to leave. "Let's just go."

"You mocking me, boy?" Mr. Boone said, this time addressing me.

"No, sir," I answered.

He glared at me for several seconds before he spoke. "*I'll* tell my kid when he can leave and when he can't."

"Yes, sir."

His glazed eyes shifted back to Boone. "You know, maybe if you spent a little more time with your brother and a little less time with your girl-friend here, you wouldn't be such a fucking pussy."

We both stood frozen, uncertain of what to say or do. Boone was mortified, of course, and I was mortified for him, but this was typical behavior when it came to his father, and as unpleasant as it was, we'd grown somewhat used to his drunken nonsense.

"Big kid like you should be playing football." His father coughed then hacked up a ball of phlegm and spit it not far from where we were standing. "Go on, get out of here," he said, plopping himself down on the bottom step. "Not that you ever miss a meal, you fat bastard, but be home for dinner tonight. Your mother's making meatloaf."

"OK, seeya, Dad," Boone said, as if all was right with the world. He gave a slight wave to his father and together we turned and headed back in the direction we'd come.

"Sorry," he said once we were out of earshot.

I patted him on the back as we walked. "Don't worry about it, man."

We were quiet for a time, just walking and thinking, or maybe trying not to think at all just then.

"So," Boone eventually said, "you hear the one about the midget fucking a giraffe?"

I laughed and his face lit up, releasing the pain and embarrassment and embracing acceptance instead.

Moving nonchalantly to the middle of the street, Boone turned, looked at me and offered a mischievous grin. "You know what time it is?"

"Oh, no."

He nodded and struck a sudden comic pose reminiscent of Elvis Presley. It was only one of the over-the-top comedic impersonations in his arsenal, but one he saved for those times when we needed a laugh the most. "Ladies and gentlemen...topless Elvis."

"Oh, God — *no!*"

Boone peeled his shirt off, flung it in my general direction and instantly assumed the persona of Elvis, swiveling his hips about and singing into his clenched fist. As I laughed hysterically, he stopped singing as suddenly as he'd begun and pointed at me. "What the hell's the matter with you, boy?" he said in a bad Elvis voice. "Ya got titties bigger than your mama's! Well — thank ya ver-ay much!"

I was laughing so hard tears had filled my eyes. "Stop, man, I can't breathe."

Waving to a crowd only he could see Boone sauntered over to where his shirt had landed and put it back on. "Come on, let's get the hell out of here before I do it again."

We spent the remainder of the afternoon in my

backyard that day, talking, hanging out, laughing; just being kids. Kids on the verge of something else, because despite the hideous encounter with Boone's father, that day was my last as a real child. For childhood to exist, there must also be innocence, and innocence — my innocence and Angela's innocence — was about to die a horrible, violent death.

That summer of 1979, Angela, only a few months beyond her twelfth birthday, was already far more accomplished than I was. She had beauty, brains, an inherent sensitivity and a gregarious nature that attracted others to her. She was an outstanding student and very popular with peers and teachers alike, and though still a child, she managed to combine the innocence of youth with the common sense normally found in those much older. We had always been close, and while we remained that way, as we approached our teenage years something in our relationship changed, a shifting of power perhaps, and by the time I had reached fifteen and Angela twelve, all the hopes and dreams Uncle and my mother had for us began to focus almost exclusively on her.

It was a bitter pill to swallow at times but made perfect sense. I wanted to be a writer, and while they were both supportive and rooted for me in their own ways, I knew they also often dismissed my dream as just that — a dream — something that would at one point or another eventually have to be traded in for reality. Angela wanted to be a lawyer. That career path was not only possible; it was probable. It was real.

"Always bet the favorite," Uncle often said. "Underdogs are underdogs for a reason, Andy. They're dreamers, and most dreamers are losers."

Regardless, I thought I'd have plenty of time to dream that summer, to indulge my fantasies of one day writing a great novel, to be able to spend hours at my typewriter escaping into worlds of my own creation. The days were longer after all, the pace slower and less stressful than during the school year.

But there would be no room for dreams that summer.

Only nightmares.

3

"How well did you know your uncle, Mr. DeMarco?"

I looked beyond the detective, across the small lobby to the windows at the front of the building. The gray sky threatened snow but was still spitting the same drizzling rain that had been falling when I'd arrived. "I haven't seen him in years."

"As I mentioned on the telephone, this *is* a murder investigation."

I stuffed my hands into my coat pockets. "Can you tell me what happened or not?"

"He was found with another man in a parked car over by the town dump. Both had been shot, executed gangland style." The detective gave a bored sigh. "That's about all I can say at this time."

"Tell me, was he still living in that apartment over on Bay Street? I can't remember the number but it was right by the water, a second-floor apartment above a bicycle shop."

"Nope." The detective consulted his clipboard

and the paperwork there. "We have his residence listed as forty-four Franklin Avenue. Our records indicate he's used that as his permanent address for the last ten years. Shared the place with his live-in girlfriend, Louise Sutherland." He looked up from the paperwork and smirked the way cops sometimes do when they mention someone they consider unsavory.

If she'd lived with Uncle for a decade, odds were she was.

"Why didn't she do the I.D.?" I asked.

"She declined."

"I don't blame her."

The detective shrugged. None of this meant a goddamn thing to him, and he didn't care if I knew it. This was some extra paperwork and a bit of overtime, not much else. I figured the way he saw it, when someone like my uncle was murdered there was just one less piece of trash in the world he had to deal with, so there wasn't anything to be particularly upset about. "I know how unpleasant this kind of thing is," he said with the bored sincerity of a telemarketer. "Appreciate your time. We're sorry for your loss."

I nodded absently and wandered into the rain.

* * *

The humidity was brutal that day, growing to unbearable heights even before morning had turned to afternoon. In anticipation the world became unnaturally still, and even the ocean breeze that normally swept through the small section of forest behind our house was eerily absent. Only the heat itself remained in motion, growing more powerful with each passing moment. Rising in rippling waves from paved and dirt roads alike, it blurred the sky and clung to the skin like a moist film.

I had spent the morning at the picnic table writing a new story, but by early afternoon I could no longer take it, and was preparing to go inside to seek refuge in some cool corner of the house when I saw Angela drift into the yard as if from thin air.

She had gone to the beach earlier that morning with a few of her friends and now stood looking like a lost waif, dirt smeared across her face, shoulders and thighs. She looked impossibly tiny to me at that moment, abnormally vulnerable somehow, and her eyes did not possess their usual sparkle. There was an aura of darkness about them I had never seen before, like something sinister had settled behind them without her permission. Her lips were dry and a bit chapped. I noticed them part, like she planned to say something, but instead she looked away as if she'd forgotten the words.

"What happened to you?" I asked.

"Nothing," she said softly.

"You're all dirty."

She brushed a straggle of hair from her face and tucked it behind her ear with exaggerated care. Her affectations were self-conscious and unfamiliar, like she had borrowed them from someone else and was just then putting them to use for the first time, and her face held the expression of someone for whom

GREG F. GIFUNE

without warning, the world had become an alien, troubling place.

"I cut through the path on my way home from the beach," she told me, which explained why she had emerged from the trees behind the house. "I fell down."

I noticed the strap on her pink one-piece bathing suit was torn and had been tied back together in an effort to hold it secure. "Better not let Mom see that, bathing suits are expensive."

Angela nodded grimly, her bottom lip protruding and trembling.

"She won't be that mad, Angie," I said. "You don't have to cry."

Without response she turned and headed for the back door. I watched her cross the yard and noticed she was moving rather gingerly. "Did you hurt yourself when you fell?" I called after her. "You sure you're OK?"

She slipped into the house like a zombie, eyes fixed straight ahead and arms dangling lifelessly at her sides. I followed her to make sure she was all right, but by the time I had gathered my papers and carried my typewriter inside, Angela had already gotten into the shower.

I found my mother at the kitchen table balancing the checkbook.

"Mom, I think Angela's sick or something."

"You what, sweetie?" she said in a distant tone, her nose still buried in the checkbook. "This damn thing *never* comes out like the statement. Never."

"Angela," I said again.

37

"She went to the beach with her friends." She continued staring at the numbers, a pen resting in the corner of her mouth. "If you're going to take a shower, Andy, do it, don't leave the water running like that."

"Angela's in the shower, that's what I'm trying to tell you."

She stabbed the register with a finger. "Ah-ha! There's one I missed, I bet that's why I couldn't get—"

"Mom," I said, louder this time. "You're not even listening to me."

She sat back, flashed me an annoyed look. "Honey, what is it? Can't you see I'm right in the middle of something here?"

"I said, I think Angela's sick."

"Angela?" Her expression changed, as though she were waiting for a translation of what I'd said into her native tongue. "Why, what's wrong?"

"She just got back from the beach and she's acting all weird."

My mother pushed the checkbook and accompanying paperwork aside, rubbed her eyes and stifled a yawn. "Weird how? What do you mean, weird?"

"She was all dirty and she said she fell. She was sort of limping."

"Angela fell? Jesus, Andy, why didn't you tell me that? Is she all right?"

"I don't know, I mean—yeah, I think so, but— Mom, I was trying to tell you."

Instead of answering me she moved down the short hallway just off the kitchen to the bathroom where Angela was showering. With a final annoyed look in my direction, she let herself in and quietly closed the door behind her.

I sat at the table, waiting, listening, perspiring in the awful humidity, and even then wrestling with the jumble of thoughts cluttering my mind.

After a moment the shower shut off and gave way to muffled voices. I stood up and walked slowly to the head of the hallway just as the bathroom door opened. My mother poked her head out. Her eyes were brimming with tears. "Mom?" I said helplessly. "What's the matter?"

"Call Uncle," she said. "Tell him to get over here as soon as he can."

"Is Angela OK?"

"Damn it, Andy, just do as I ask!"

The door closed and I stood there stupidly as silence returned to the house, an awful, unearthly silence.

After a moment, I walked back into the kitchen and reached for the wall phone.

4

It felt good to be out in the fresh air again, even though the drizzle turned to an icy, pouring rain the moment I stepped outside. I put on my old fedora and stood in the desolate parking lot a while, probably from a distance looking like some mysterious stranger in an old movie. Sans movie, I suppose that's exactly what I was. Standing alongside my car and battling my typical feelings of estrangement from the world, I listened to the rhythmic cadence of freezing drops pelt my coat and hat. Hands stuffed in my trench coat, I recalled the morning prior and watched my breath trail off in cloudy spirals as it tumbled from my nostrils and mouth.

I had been safely insulated at home with Martha and the cats. A Sunday, I had spent the morning in my sweatpants and a t-shirt, sitting on the couch with a hot cup of tea and a novel. A light and playful Vivaldi tune played on the stereo, and in the space between my chest, where the book was resting, and my lap, where my cup and saucer were resting, two seven-week-old kittens, Benny and Boo, playfully wrestled with each other. Martha and I had found a litter of four kittens abandoned in the woods near our home during one of our evening walks. Two had already died but two were clinging to life. We buried the dead and took the others in, as we had with other stray or abandoned animals over the years, and after a few weeks of successful bottle-feeding, numerous veterinarian visits, and constant nurturing, the kittens not only survived, they flourished. Rather than finding them good homes elsewhere, we decided to keep these two, and finally healthy, we were just beginning to enjoy their company, and they ours.

Across from me in a comfortable chair reading the newspaper, Martha sat with her legs beneath her, unaware of her grace and beauty. Later we would make love in the shower, have breakfast, go for a walk then lie on the couch and enjoy our day off, snuggling with the new additions to our family. We would watch movies and let the day slip past as if unnoticed, in silence. These quiet times were what I lived for, the moments when Martha and I existed together yet apart, in love and alive in a seductively meaningful place that existed somewhere just beneath the surface of everyday life and all the confines that came with it.

We were alive. Gently.

It had taken me years to find this place in the world, to renovate it and nurture it, and in sharing it with the woman I loved, transform it from a fantasy to what I had always dreamed it might be.

And one phone call had interrupted and sent it spiraling downward, crashing into thousands of pieces, those shards threatening to turn the present into some parallel vision of the past, a black mirror reflecting that which I had presumed long dead. Fatally wounded, I had left it to die, and now, violently, it had returned from the darkness like a ghoul in a horror story.

You pretentious pussy, a voice said from somewhere behind me. *Always remember, Andy, there's the way you want the world to be...and the way it just fucking is.*

The words were so clear I actually turned, expecting to see Uncle standing there. But there was only a cold rain slowly turning to snow.

I let the memories of Sunday slip away with the winter wind, climbed into my car and headed for my uncle's last known address.

* * *

About fifteen minutes after a frantic and confusing phone call, during which I was unable to report much of anything in the way of significant information, Uncle arrived and stormed into the kitchen with a worried scowl on his normally pleasant face. "What the hell kind of call was that? You didn't make any sense, what's going on?"

"I don't know, I—"

"Where's Angela?"

"Upstairs with Mom."

He turned and headed up the stairs, joining my mother and Angela in her bedroom and leaving me frightened and confused at the kitchen table. Within seconds I heard muffled voices trickling down the staircase but couldn't make out any specific words.

No longer able to contain my curiosity, I quietly climbed the stairs, cognizant of each squeaking step, and crouched in the hallway just outside Angela's bedroom door.

I could hear Angela sobbing and Uncle's voice questioning her interspersed with sporadic interruptions from my mother. This went on for quite a while, but I could still only make out every third or fourth word.

I'd been straining to hear and concentrating so hard that when my mother and Uncle emerged from the bedroom I didn't have time to make an escape. Instead, as they quietly closed Angela's bedroom door behind them, I leaned against the wall with arms folded casually and asked, "What's going on?"

My mother wiped tears from her eyes, smudging eyeliner into thick black splotches across her cheeks like war paint. "Go outside for a while," she said in a dismissive tone.

"Is Angie OK?"

"Go outside for a while." She spun toward me so forcefully I thought for a moment she might hit me. Then, realizing how I had interpreted her abrupt motion, she reached out tenderly and cupped the side of my face. "Go outside. Uncle and I need to talk."

Before I could object she descended the stairs.

As Uncle followed he whispered, "Stay close to home."

I took my time on the stairs, crossed the kitchen slowly and pretended to slam shut the screen door as they met in the adjacent den. Out of sight, I inched closer, lingering just beyond the open door and heard ice clink glass as Uncle mixed drinks for them both.

"Marie, maybe you should just call the cops."

"Never thought I'd hear that from *you*."

"Yeah, but under the circumstances it's probably best."

"And what are they going to do besides put that poor little girl through hell all over again? Besides, the sonofabitch is a minor, nothing will happen to him. It boils down to his word against—"

"She's twelve, for Christ's sake. They got tests that'll show she's been violated."

My throat cinched shut and it suddenly felt as if my stomach would burst.

"And he'll get a slap on the wrist and you know it."

"Marie, calm down a minute and try to think about this."

"Don't fucking tell me to calm down."

"Whether he gets a slap on the wrist or not, that's beside the point right now. You've still got to get Angie to a doctor. If you want to keep it quiet, I know a guy."

"Some back alley hack? Sounds wonderful. But what about this Michael Ring?"

A small burst of bile sprayed into the bottom of

my throat. I choked it back.

"What about him?"

"I want to do something."

"Like what?"

"Like kill the little bastard."

The silence that followed seemed to last an eternity as countless thoughts flooded my mind and I attempted to sort them into something approaching a coherent order.

"You know I can't do that," Uncle finally said.

"I only know you *won't.*"

"Take it easy."

"You take it easy. I want him dead. I want you to cut his cock off and choke him with it. Use your connections, put some of those scumbags you know to work on it if you have to but I want him dead. I want him fucking dead." Her voice broke as anger erupted into tears. "That sonofabitch! That goddamn sonofabitch!"

"Listen to me," Uncle said. "If you don't want to involve the cops in this then I can...I can *handle* it, OK?"

"Then do it."

"But I can't kill this kid."

"Why not?"

"I know you're in a rage right now and you deserve to be—shit, so am I—but you have to try to use your head here. This isn't the movies or some book. You're talking about murder, and you don't want that on your head. Trust me."

"I couldn't give a shit less."

"And secondly, Angela is still alive."

"This is me you're talking to, Paulie, not the kids. You don't have to play the hero for me so just spare me your street ethics, all right? That asshole dragged my little girl into the woods and — that poor innocent little baby, he — "

"Marie, it's not that easy. If you go that route no one can know what happened, understand? You said it didn't look like she has any serious physical damage, but we'll take Angie to that doctor I know and let him check her out to be sure. Any other doctor's gonna have to report it, and we can't have that. Nobody can know a thing, and we'll have to talk to Angela and make sure she understands no one can ever know what happened to her. No one. If anybody finds out, and something should happen to this Ring asshole, the first place they're gonna come looking is your house and mine."

"I don't care how we have to do it," she said evenly. "I want him dead."

"What the hell do you think I am, for Christ's sake, some psycho who goes around murdering people?"

Silence answered.

With my heart thudding against my chest I slipped out through the kitchen door into the backyard, the world a watery blur. I don't know how long I sat at the picnic table trying to quell my tears and grab hold of a clear thought, only that it was Uncle's sudden presence that snapped me back to reality.

"Did you hear what we were saying?" he asked.

I pawed the tears from my eyes and looked at

him. "Is Angela going to be all right?"

He pulled a pack of cigarettes from his inside jacket pocket, tapped one free of the pack and rolled it into the corner of his mouth. "What do *you* think?"

I knew the answer. She would never — could never — be the same, and while I wanted desperately to feel the rage my mother was experiencing I could only marshal profound sorrow. Nothing we did, nothing we said would ever change things or save Angela from what had already happened. "What are we going to do?"

"We're going for a ride," Uncle said, lighting his cigarette. "You and me."

"How come?"

He inhaled deeply then released the smoke through his nose. "You know a kid named Michael Ring?"

"I go to school with him," I said, trying my best to control the sick feeling in the pit of my stomach. "We're in the same grade."

"You know where he lives?"

"Yeah."

He nodded. "Then show me."

5

By the time I reached Franklin Avenue the rain had completely turned to a heavy wet snow. Even a working-class town like Warden couldn't help but look beautiful and somehow magical draped in white. When I lived there as a kid, Warden was a constantly growing town struggling even then to maintain its identity. But now it was a full-fledged little city, and in its evolution had traded charm, warmth, familiarity and its individuality for the expediency and soulless flash that littered nearly every other town across the country. Even the main drag looked different. Most of the small businesses that existed there years before were gone, and those that remained were chains rather than the independently owned shops they'd once been. Where the quaint old General Store had been now stood a flashy convenience store with two rows of gas pumps out front, and the drugstore where Boone and I had spent our lawn-mowing money was now a video store with huge front windows covered in movie posters and gaudy signage.

Mickey's Diner had survived, but it too had undergone some substantial renovation and now more closely resembled a generic family restaurant than the stylized diner of yesteryear it had once been.

Franklin was a short jog of an avenue off the main drag, one of those neighborhoods that had been stranded between its more rural past and the urban present, a smattering of old homes and a couple apartment building holdouts sandwiched between acres of commercial property. Forty-four was an apartment building, and since the detective had not given me an apartment number, I found myself sitting in my parked car with both hands resting atop the wheel, watching the snow fall and contemplating my next move.

The building itself looked dark and quiet, but it was only a two-story, so I knew it couldn't house too many units. I waited several minutes but no one came or went, so I climbed from the car and tramped carefully across the small front lawn. While still several feet away I noticed a line of mail slots to the right of the front door. The third from the top was marked: *Sutherland*. Once on the steps I looked for buzzers or a doorbell but came up empty. On a whim, I tried the door. It was unlocked.

I stepped into a small, dark hallway. As my eyes adjusted to my surroundings I removed my hat and brushed the snow from it, then moved deeper into the building. The first floor had what appeared to be two apartments, one to my immediate left and one directly in front of me. Neither door was marked, so

I decided to try both.

After knocking on the first door twice without any luck, I turned to try the second, when I heard a series of locks disengaging, and it opened slightly, still secured by a small chain. I cocked my head and squinted through the minimal light in an attempt to better make out the face peering through the few inches of space the chain allowed.

"Can I help you?"

I moved a bit closer and saw an elderly woman. "I'm sorry to bother you, but I'm looking for Louise Sutherland."

"I'm the landlord here." The old woman's eyes narrowed suspiciously. "What is this regarding?"

"My name's Andrew DeMarco. Ms. Sutherland lived here with my Uncle Paul."

"Paulie?" she asked in a softer tone. "You're Paulie's nephew?"

"Yes, ma'am."

The door closed in my face but seconds later I heard the chain slide free. The door slowly swung open and a petite woman in a housecoat and slippers appeared. She looked as if she'd been napping. "Miriam Waters," she said, extending a hand. "I'm so sorry to hear about your uncle."

I took her hand in mine. It was skeletal and cool to the touch. "Thank you."

"We just got the news yesterday."

"Yes," I said. "Me too."

She wrapped her arms around herself as if cold. "Such a horrible thing."

I nodded, unsure of how to respond.

"He was a very nice man," the woman told me.

"I was hoping to speak with Ms. Sutherland."

"Of course." She peeked about the hallway dramatically, I assumed to make certain we were alone. "Poor Louise, they've been together a long time," she said just above a whisper. "I told her she should take a few days off and give herself a chance to come to terms with all of this, but she insisted on going to work. Keeps her mind busy, I suppose, but she was so upset last night. I was up quite late with her, just talking. Well, listening mostly."

"Is she at work now, Ms. Waters?"

"*Miriam*," she said, patting my arm like the grandmother she probably was.

"Miriam," I repeated.

"Have you ever heard of a gentlemen's club called *The Blue Slipper*?"

"No, ma'am, I'm afraid not."

"Not sure why they call it that." She arched an eyebrow with conspiratorial glee. "There hasn't been a gentlemen anywhere near that place since they built it."

I nearly broke a smile as she gave me directions.

* * *

Uncle and I had been parked next to the General Store, across the street and a few doors down from Michael Ring's house, for more than an hour. The house was bigger than ours but more rundown, with a weed-infested front yard surrounded by a waist-high chain-link fence. The air was thick and stagnant, the sun blinding within the confines of Uncle's car. He sat next to me quietly smoking a cigarette; eyes focused on the stretch of road while a thin film of perspiration beaded across his forehead. I had done my best to appear calm and collected, but my heart was still racing and my stomach was in knots.

"What's the deal with this punk?" Uncle asked.

"What do you mean?"

"What do you know about him?"

I wiped some sweat from my forehead with the back of my hand and tried to separate my knowledge of Michael Ring from the rest of the madness filling my head. "I go to school with him. He—"

"Who lives in that house with him? Both parents?"

"Yeah."

"What's his old man do?"

"I don't know, I—I don't know him, really, I—"

"Does he have any brothers or sisters?"

"No."

"Anybody in his family I need to worry about? Any cops in the family, or lawyers, that kind of thing?"

"I don't know, I don't think so."

"Don't *think*, Andy. You either know or you don't know."

"I don't know."

Uncle puffed his cigarette. "I'll check into him."

I watched him a moment, but could not read his face. He didn't look angry, rather quiet and composed to the point of near docility. "What are we going to do?"

"It'll be OK." His face hinted at a smile as he reached over and gave my leg a firm pat. "We're gonna do what we have to do."

I was about to ask what exactly that entailed when I saw Michael Ring turn the corner, dribbling a basketball and strutting along with his usual arrogant smirk. He was tall and muscular for his age, with a ruggedly handsome face and long hair he kept secured with a cotton headband.

"That's him," I heard myself say. "The one with the basketball."

Uncle sighed, and there was a subtle change in his expression. He leaned across me and popped open the glove compartment, removed an object wrapped in dark cloth and pushed it into my hand without uttering a word.

I felt its weight and reluctantly peeled back the cloth to reveal a pair of shiny brass knuckles. "What am I supposed to..." I looked at him but he was staring straight ahead. "You want me to *fight* him?"

"If I touch him I'll have the cops all over me. If you go after him it's just two young guys having a fight." Finally, he turned to me. "You walk right up, you don't say anything and you don't look him in the eye. You walk right up and you hit him as hard as you can dead in the center of his face, *cabeesh*? Go for his nose. You'll snap it easy. There'll be a lot of blood, and it'll probably squirt like a bastard, so take a step back and to the side. He'll be reeling, trust me. Once you move to the side, you hit him again.

Right here." He jabbed a finger against his temple. "Hard as you can. He'll go down faster than a five-dollar whore. Once he's down, you open your fist slow and let the knuckles slip free into your other hand. You hold them down to your side, and you do it slow and casual, so it doesn't look to anybody watching like you used anything except your fist, OK? Then once he's down, you get a good sturdy stance and you kick him three times, real hard. Once in the gut, twice in the balls. He's gonna start coughing and gagging and all that, but don't be afraid, you won't kill him. After the third kick you crouch down and grab him by that long hair of his. Jerk his head back so your mouth is right next to his ear, and you whisper—make sure you don't say it loud—you tell him you know what he did to your sister, and this is only the beginning if he tries to cause more trouble. You tell him the next time you'll kill him. *Next time, motherfucker, I'll kill you.* Say it just like that, but quiet, calm. I'll park around the corner before all this, so when you're done you walk—*don't run*—over to the car and get in. You don't do anything else and you don't say anything else. You walk up the block and get in the car nice and easy, like it's no big deal and we drive away. There aren't many people around anyway, but if somebody sees all they'll know is you had a fight and just walked away. If anybody asks later, you guys had a fight. He said some shit to you at school or something—make something up but leave Angela out of it, understand? You hit him a couple times then left, it was no big deal, and you don't admit you hit him with anything but your fist, understand? If he's hurt, well, you don't know anything about that. You just punched him a couple times and he fell down but he was fine when you left."

I laughed a little, not because there was anything remotely funny about the situation but because I didn't know what else to do. "Uncle, I can't — I can't do all that."

"Take a look at him and think about what he did to your sister. Think about Angie."

I tried to swallow but gagged. I had been in three fistfights in my entire life, and though Uncle had taught me how to handle myself, Michael Ring was physically much larger than I was and had a reputation at school as being a tough kid. I had seen him fight on several occasions at school and had never seen him come anywhere near losing. Most kids at school were terrified of him. "We should go to the police." I dropped the brass knuckles on the seat between us. "He should be arrested for what he did and — "

"Did you hear a word I said?"

"Uncle, I'm…"

"What, afraid?"

I nodded.

"It's OK to be afraid, Andy. We're all afraid now and then. But there's a difference between being afraid and being a coward." He took a final drag on his cigarette and flicked it out the window. "Which one are you? You afraid? Or are you a coward?"

I squinted through the glare of the sun; saw

Michael standing across the street, the sound of his basketball slapping pavement echoing in my ears.

"*Please*, Uncle," I said, hating how weak my voice sounded. "I don't want to do this."

"Then get the fuck out of the car."

"What? I—"

"You heard me."

"But Uncle—"

The sudden look in his eyes stopped me in mid-sentence. It was cold and lifeless, almost evil. "Don't worry about it," he said softly. "Just get out of the car, Andy."

I pushed open the door and stepped out, my head swimming.

"Forget you were ever here." Uncle slid his sunglasses on. "Think you can handle that much?"

But for Michael Ring, the street was virtually empty. Nothing seemed real anymore.

I watched from the parking lot as Uncle pulled away and drove to the corner where Michael was standing. He asked for directions to the town hall, and before Michael could make his way to the car to respond I turned, and in a panic, ran in the opposite direction, unaware of where I was headed—or why—only knowing I had to get as far away from there as I could. I never looked back. Not once.

6

The Blue Slipper was located near the town industrial park and not far from the waterfront. Ironically,
it was only a few blocks from the apartment where
Uncle lived when I was younger. The neighborhood
had never been a particularly spectacular one, but in
the years since I'd left it had grown worse. Dirty
and grim, it was a remote street with mostly old
textile mills and fish processing plants — the two
largest employers in Warden — mixed with a handful
of rough-looking bars, an adult book and video store
and the club where Louise Sutherland worked.

I pulled into the parking lot but left the engine
running so I could continue to employ the car heater.
The Blue Slipper was a tan building, once white
perhaps, built low to the ground and straight back
from the road, with a flat roof and squared corners
that reminded me of an enormous shoebox. A set of
black double doors stood ominously on the face of
the building and on the roof a neon blue slipper that
looked more like a spike-heeled pump blinked in

timed intervals beneath a painted sign advertising the name. No windows, no other visible doors.

A sudden vibration on my belt caught my attention. I slipped my cell phone free. My home number scrolled across the digital display. "Martha?"

"Hi." Her voice was tentative, delicate. "They said on the news that area of the coast was in for quite a snowstorm, I just wanted to make sure you got there safely."

"The snow just started." I pictured her at home, draped in kittens and a blanket from the couch, sitting in her favorite chair in the den. "I'm here," I told her. "I'm OK."

Her breath whispered through the phone. "How's your mother holding up?"

"I haven't seen her yet."

"Oh."

"I plan to a bit later. I just left the morgue."

"God." She sighed.

"Yeah." I watched snow fall across the neon slipper. "How are the babies?"

The mere mention of the kittens brightened her tone. "Great. They played themselves out a few minutes ago and they're asleep now, all cuddled up together."

I wanted to drive away right then and there and go back home. A part of me still wishes I had. "I'm not sure about the funeral arrangements yet. Angela's supposed to be getting in tonight, so once we're settled in at Mom's and I know more I'll give you a call, OK?"

"I wish you'd let me come with you," she said softly. "I feel like I should be there."

"It's better this way, trust me. I'll be home soon, sweetheart."

"You do what you have to do. This is family."

You're my family, I thought. *These are ghosts.*

* * *

I ran the entire three miles to my house without stopping before I finally collapsed against a neighbor's stonewall. I knew my mother was home, knew I should go inside and warn her about what was happening but couldn't bring myself to do it.

I spent the next several hours that afternoon walking, thinking, wanting to go back home but too afraid of what I might find once I got there to actually do so. Every time a car drove by or a voice echoed across the street from passersby, I expected to find Uncle there, telling me it had all been a bad joke and to get back into the car so we could go home. But he never came, and it was nearly dark when I finally crept in through the kitchen door.

My mother and Angela were asleep upstairs, cuddled together like two undisturbed flowers beneath the serene eye of an otherwise violent storm. They looked so peaceful it seemed impossible any harm could come to either of them, and all the more perverse and dreadful that it had. I studied them in silence for several minutes, unable to convince myself to wake them.

To that point I felt I needed to work things out on

my own. This was a personal issue, one that I had no right to take outside our family circle, such as it was, but Boone was the closest thing I had to a brother and it seemed to me all bets were off. After staring at the kitchen phone for an eternity, I picked it up and dialed his house.

"Can you meet me down at the park?" I asked when he came to the phone.

"Now? It's getting dark out. Monsters and shit."

"This is serious, I need to talk to you."

"So go ahead. First time using a phone there, Einstein?"

"Boone, I'm not kidding around, this is really fucking serious."

I could almost see him frowning into the phone, contorting his face the way he often did when confronted with something he couldn't deflect or allay with humor. "What's the matter, Andy?"

"Can you get out of the house or not?"

"Yeah, I guess. My Dad's passed out and my Mom won't give a shit."

"The park in ten minutes, OK?"

"I'll be there."

And he was. The park, better known as Smyth Park, had been named after one of the town's foundering fathers back in colonial times, and was really more a field than a park. Years before it had been a place where small independent carnivals and circuses stopped and set up shop on their New England tours, and where the town held little league baseball games. But over the years the public school fields and ballparks had replaced Smyth Park, reducing it to a large, often empty field with a rotting baseball diamond and backstop at one end, and an equally dilapidated concession stand at the other. To discourage people from driving cars into the park, particularly teenagers who for a time had used it as a make-out spot, the dirt roads leading in and out were roped off and purposely left unpaved and rutted. But for occasional walkers or kids who still played there now and then during daylight hours, Smyth Park was generally deserted. Since electricity had not been fed to the park in eons, at night, it was pitch black there. But in summer darkness fell slowly, and coupled with a bright moon, the area was easily negotiable.

I leaned against the rotted concession stand until I heard the rattling of Boone's bicycle as he sped along the bumpy entrance road. I waved to him as his bike turned and headed for me.

He came to an abrupt halt in the grass a few feet away, winded from what had obviously been a breakneck pace. His bicycle looked tiny beneath his large frame, comical. "Andy?" he huffed, climbing off his bike and discarding it. It rattled on for a few feet then tipped over, the rear wheel still spinning. "Dude, it's gonna be totally dark soon. This place gives me the creeps, especially at night. What'd we have to come way out here for?"

It was a fair question. There were plenty of other, more convenient places we could have met in town, places where we could have benefited from privacy. But I wanted the approaching darkness here, the barrenness, and the cover it provided. I wanted to hide away until daylight returned, bringing with it clarity and reason and sanity.

"I figured nobody else would be around and we could talk in private."

"We coulda talked in private out in front of my fucking house, shit-for-brains. Didn't have to come out here for that." Boone wiped perspiration from his forehead with the back of his hand. He looked as disheveled as ever in a white t-shirt stained from dinner, a pair of shorts and sneakers with no socks. "Hate this place," he said. I could tell by the way he was squinting through the dying light that he was trying to see my face more clearly, and then from his expression, that he had. "Jesus, Andy, you OK?"

"I don't think so, man." Emotion pooled at the base of my throat as all the events of the day burst free in a single frantic surge. "Some bad shit happened today."

7

It took at least a full minute for my eyes to adjust to the dim lighting beyond the front doors of *The Blue Slipper*. I stood in a narrow vestibule dripping snow and rainwater onto a cheap industrial red carpet smattered with cigarette burns and various small tears. Music played somewhere nearby, the rhythmic thud of a baseline vibrating the floor. A cigarette machine sat to my right beneath a poster advertising the headlining dancer that week, a platinum blonde with a cartoon-like figure. Ignoring the reek of cigarettes and cheap booze, I followed the hallway entrance to a small glass-encased booth with an open window in front. Inside, a woman on a stool stared at the counter before her as if in a trance, only looking up when I was within a foot or two of the booth itself. Beyond her glass closet was a bar and runway stage where a bored-looking topless woman in a g-string gyrated to the music for a handful of men seated throughout the bar and table area. It was equally dark there, as along with the backlight from the bar, small candles encased in red glass on each table provided the only light.

The woman in the glass booth stared at me for a moment without speaking then jerked a thumb at a small sign next to her that advertised the cover charge. She looked too old to be working in a strip club, yet possessed the weathered, experienced look of someone who knew the score, knew the streets and the characters that inhabited them because she was one herself. "Fifteen bucks," she said in a raspy, smoker's voice.

Though I'd never laid eyes on her before I somehow knew who she was. "I'm looking for Louise Sutherland."

She sighed and shook her head, her onyx dangle earrings swaying. "You new? Thought I knew all the cops on the force these days."

"I'm not a cop."

"What do you want?" Her eyes were large, brown, and saddled with dark bags, and her makeup was a bit heavy but did little to cover how truly tired she looked. At one time this had been a stunningly beautiful woman, and despite her palpable exhaustion, traces of that beauty still remained.

I pulled off my hat, held it down by my side. Rainwater trickled across the bridge of my nose. I wiped it free. "I'm Andy DeMarco," I told her. "Paul's nephew."

Recognition of my name dawned across her face, and she self-consciously ran her fingers through her short hair, combing a few thick strands off her forehead. I could almost hear the wheels turning in her head. "I...I'm Louise."

"I was hoping maybe we could talk."

She nodded absently, like her mind was racing, already jumping ahead. "Yeah," she finally said. "Sure, of—of course."

She slid down off the stool slowly, with more effort than it should've taken, and walked out of the booth through a back door. I watched as she crossed to the bar, leaned over and said something to the bartender. He nodded, signaled to another employee, and that man followed Louise back to the booth and took her place on the stool. He glanced at me long enough to let me know he'd seen and made a mental image of me, but otherwise seemed completely disinterested in my presence. Louise reached under the counter, retrieved a clutch-purse, slipped into a long black coat then joined me on the free side of the glass.

From her hairstyle to her wardrobe, Louise Sutherland had the look of a woman better suited to the late 1940s or early 1950s. She wore a simple but clingy black dress that sported quite a bit of cleavage and stopped just above her knees, nylons and spike heels that struck me as something one might wear to a dinner party rather than a day job on a stool at a skin bar. I guessed she was in her middle forties to early fifties, but couldn't be certain which end of that spectrum she fell into. Her life had not been an easy one, and it was evident in her face. She was not overweight by any stretch of the imagination, but neither was she particularly skinny, with a busty, hourglass figure that looked as dated as the rest of her persona. There was an air of overt sexuality about her, of unmistakable femininity mixed with a harder exterior, all of which she seemed wholly unaware of. Or perhaps she was all too aware, and years of practice only made it appear that way. As she came closer the smell of perfume and makeup wafted from her in a slow wave.

"There's a little place right around the corner," she said. "We can get some coffee."

It wasn't until we got outside that I realized how stifling the heat had been inside. Louise walked a few paces ahead of me, noticeably surprised to find it had begun to snow. My eyes watered in the cold air, blurring my view. I followed her to the end of the block and across a narrow side street, her heels clicking pavement and our breath trailing and swirling about us like freshly expelled spirits.

Louise led me to a small café sandwiched between an unoccupied and rundown storefront and an equally dilapidated pawnshop. A counter with stools overlooking a grill filled the back wall, and a few tables were lined along the front window. It struck me as peculiar that there would be such a large window in a place so dreary, the view through which consisted of another vacant and decayed building covered in graffiti.

As we entered, a rotund man in a stained apron waved his spatula at us from behind the counter then turned back to his grill. A couple of old men sat huddled on stools, but all the tables were empty.

Louise chose one in the far corner. As I helped her off with her coat then took the chair opposite her, an awkward silence passed between us.

From her purse Louise pulled a cigarette case and a matching lighter. Rather than make direct eye contact with me she looked out the window at a neighborhood on its last leg. "Do you drink coffee?"

"Sure."

"How do you take it?"

"Black."

She opened the case and slid a cigarette free. Her fingernails were manicured and painted blood red, which contrasted oddly with her black dress. "Freddy," she called to the man at the grill, her face still turned to the window, "couple black coffees when you get a chance."

"You got it, Lou," he called back.

Louise slipped the cigarette between her lips, snapped shut the case and placed it on the table between us. Several seconds passed before she lit it, and when she did she took a slow drag, held the smoke in her lungs for a beat then exhaled gradually. As she plucked the cigarette from her mouth I noticed a lipstick stain along the filter. She smoked in silence a while longer with a precision and fluidity that seemed nearly religious in its execution. She began to relax, her posture softening with each new drag, and I found myself mesmerized until Freddy slapped two mugs of steaming coffee on the table. When he moved away Louise finally turned from the window and gathered her mug closer. "The coffee's not bad but stay away from the food."

The clearer light revealed eyes reddened from sleeplessness and hours of crying. There was an innate toughness to this woman who had spent so many years with my uncle, a protective shield against the daily life she led, I supposed, but there was also a self-conscious vulnerability that was more than likely only detectable during times such as these, when trauma and fatigue conspired to expose the depth of her true nature.

"I'm sorry to just spring myself on you out of the blue like this," I said.

She sipped her coffee, leaving behind another lipstick stain on the rim of the mug. "Actually, it's nice to finally meet you. Just too bad it's under these circumstances."

I sat there trying to think of something to say as the steam from my mug slithered up across my chin and cheeks. Mercifully, the aroma of coffee covered the otherwise dominant stench of grease in the room. "I know you two were together a long time," I eventually managed. "I can't imagine what you must be going through, but I want you to know I appreciate you seeing me like this."

Louise gave a spasm-like smile that came and went so fast I barely noticed it.

"I just thought we should talk," I told her.

She took another pull on her cigarette, this time more forcefully, then crushed it in a small plastic ashtray. "What about?"

"I identified his body a little while ago." I expected her to say something in response. When she didn't, even though I didn't really want it, I forced down a swallow of coffee and said, "I was surprised at how different he looked. I'd forgotten I'm thirty-five myself, which made him fifty-six. I realized then how long it had been since I'd seen him. All this time, all these years seem more real, suddenly."

"Yes, they do."

I felt like a salesman who had forgotten his pitch. "Time has a way of doing that."

"That's because Time's a thief," Louise said evenly. "And like all the good ones, once you realize he's been there, he's already gone."

* * *

Boone leaned against the concession stand wall and slid slowly to the ground. He looked like I felt, like he'd been punched in the stomach. Hard. "*Whoa,*" he said, for about the fifth or sixth time since I'd finished telling him what had happened earlier.

In the silence that followed crickets buzzed joyously, oblivious to my plight and reminding me that we were the intruders here, the strangers. I envied their ability to be heard and not seen, and wanted to join them in the shelter of the tall grass surrounding us, hidden and protected in their invisibility, their concealment and the safety of their numbers.

But in that here and now there was only Boone and only me and the things we both now knew. It hadn't occurred to me until then that revealing what

I'd seen and heard that day not only relieved me of some burden, it transferred it to him. Perhaps unfairly, but such was our relationship in those days, the friendship of youth—friendship in its purist form—pitfalls and all.

"Michael Ring's always been an asshole," Boone said. "But Jesus, why would he do something like that to Angie? Sick fuck, she's just a little kid. You sure she's OK?"

"I don't know, I—I think so. They're supposed to take her to some doctor my uncle knows, some guy who'll keep it quiet like they want."

"He's so dead," Boone mumbled. "Michael Ring is *so* fucking dead."

"What am I going to do?"

He seemed puzzled. "What do you mean?"

"Boone, what if he killed him?"

He tore a piece of grass free from the field and began twisting it in his hands. Boone had always been close to Uncle too, and looked up to him as much as I did. But he had heard the stories and rumors, and knew there was mystery there, areas no one ventured to, darkness we never talked about except in carefully calculated ways, albeit in the form of hero worship.

Nobody messes with my uncle.

Yeah, your Uncle's a bad dude, he kicks ass! You think he's in the Mafia?

I don't know, man. Maybe. He doesn't talk about it.

Your uncle's so cool.

The coolest.

In an instant everything had changed. We no

longer had the luxury of whimsy, of comic book or teenage-boy versions of valor. It was more than just talk now, more than empty words, braggadocio and blood and guts fantasies as phony as a drive-in horror movie. This time it was all too real.

"He probably just kicked his ass real bad," Boone said.

"But what if he really killed him?"

Boone sat there quietly a moment. "If Michael Ring did that to Angie he fucking deserves it. Shit, if I had a sister—"

"You don't."

"But if I did, I—"

"Yeah, but you don't."

"Fine." He sighed, tossing the now mangled blade of grass aside. "My mom then. I *do* have one of those...sort of. If somebody did that to my mother I'd fucking kill them myself."

"This is real, Boone."

"Remember Ed Kelleher? Your uncle kicked the shit out of him and all he did was spank Angela. You were cool about that."

"That was years ago, and I was just little too. And—Jesus, Boone—nobody died."

"Dude, what do you care if he kills him?"

"Are you nuts?"

"Are you? He raped your sister. You should've kicked his ass when you had the chance. Shit, it woulda taken ten guys to hold me back, and you couldn't even get out of the car."

"Like I could fight with Michael Ring. He would've kicked my ass."

"So what?" Boone struggled back to his feet. "You're a man. That shit happens sometimes. At least you'd be doing the right thing."

"The right thing? Jesus, you're as bad as the rest of them. Everybody's so pissed they're not thinking about all this. No one's *thinking*."

"Seems to me you're worrying more about Michael Ring than you are about your little sister."

We were just inches apart. "Fuck you, man."

"OK whatever, get mad at me." Boone waved at me dismissively. "Yeah, that makes a lot of sense."

"Nothing's going to change what happened. No matter what I do or Uncle does or anybody does, it's not going to change what happened to Angela. It's not going to make her feel better, it's not going to make what happened to her and what she's feeling go away."

"So what? Maybe that's not even the point. He raped Angela, Andy, he—"

"I know what he did."

"He has to pay for that. He has to be punished."

"I'm not saying he shouldn't be punished. I'm not saying that what he did was OK. But they should call the police and have him arrested. He should go to jail."

"Shit. Juvenile, maybe."

"Boone, if Uncle kills him *he'll* go to jail, probably for the rest of his life. I don't want my uncle to go to prison." I turned away from him and ran my hands through my hair. They came back damp with perspiration. "And besides," I said. "It's murder."

"Maybe nothing happened," Boone said. "You

said when you took off running he was just talking to him, so maybe he didn't *do* anything."

I wanted to believe that could be true, but my gut told me different.

Boone wandered off, putting some necessary distance between us. "I don't know," he said. "I don't know what you should do."

"No matter what," I told him, "you can't say anything, Boone. Not to anyone."

He nodded.

"If something does happen, and we know about it, we could be in trouble too."

"I'd never rat," he said softly. "Ever."

I wished I could go somewhere else for a while, even if only to sit and think, but it had never been more evident than at that precise moment just how cloistered we really were. We rarely left town regardless of circumstance. We couldn't even drive yet. There was nowhere to go, and no way to get there even if there was. Warden was our entire universe, our existence a life on the head of a pin.

Darkness arrived unnoticed.

8

"Angela called me last night," Louise announced. "She's flying in tonight."

I nodded. "I'm planning to meet her over at our mother's."

Louise visibly grimaced, her pain and my mother's shared in that moment. "I'm going there later too. I don't know why the hell I went to work, I—I just couldn't spend another minute in that apartment by myself. I talked to Marie on the phone for a while but...but all we did was cry." She shrugged almost apologetically, and I wanted to reach across the table and touch her, to reassure her that there was no need for any of that.

"I'm headed to the house a bit later," I told her. "But I wanted to see you first."

"Why?"

This time I looked away. In her mind I was sure I'd deserved that. After all, she'd been with my uncle for a decade and had a relationship not only with him, but with my mother as well, and as much as one could have with Angela, who lived across the country and who returned to Warden generally only for funerals, weddings, and on occasion, for the holidays. Louise had been more a member of our family these past years than I had.

I remembered my mother telling me about some woman Uncle was with, but we rarely spoke about him when I called, and even when we did it was sparingly, so until earlier that day I'd had no idea Louise Sutherland existed in any real sense. To me, she had been someone briefly referred to in conversation with my mother or Angela over the years, a woman to whom I had dismissed and assigned the same insignificance I had labeled all of Uncle's other girlfriends with. But Louise was something different. She was real, probably the only meaningful non-plutonic relationship Uncle had ever had with a woman. And I'd missed it, missed them. I'd missed her.

"You look a lot like him," she said rather unexpectedly.

I found Louise's comment curious since she hadn't sustained a look in my direction for more than a few seconds. But she was right. I could've easily been mistaken for Uncle's son rather than his nephew.

"When he was younger, anyway," she added. She held her coffee mug like it was a baby animal, cradling it between her fingers tenderly. "I've seen pictures of you when you were little but..." her voice faded to silence. "He carried this one snapshot in his wallet of him with you and Angela. You two are standing on either side of him holding his hands. You were probably—I don't know—eight or nine, maybe, just a little fella, so Angela can't be more than five or six. He looks so happy in it. Whenever he'd talk to somebody about you or Angela he'd pull that picture out. 'Course he had more recent ones of Angela; we had them all over the house. But he didn't have any of you besides old ones. He did have a copy of your high school graduation picture, though. Your mother gave him one. I guess you'd already stopped talking to him quite a while before that, though."

Louise stared down into her coffee for a while.

"It's complicated," I told her.

Her dark eyes lifted. "I know."

I wondered just how much.

Pain and regret hung in the air between us like a gossamer curtain. I imagined Uncle holding this woman, kissing her, loving her. I imagined him laughing with her, clowning and pulling her from a chair for a quick dance around the kitchen the way he'd done with my mother so many years before. I imagined them in their apartment, lying in bed together in silence while shadows played along the walls and ceilings of their bedroom. I imagined her resting her head on his shoulder, and him wrapping his arms around her, holding her tight, and smiling the way he so often did, as if he hadn't a worry in the world and there was nowhere else he'd rather be.

"The police told me he was killed with another man," I said.

Louise gave a noncommittal nod and reached again for her cigarettes. "Yeah, that's what they told me too."

"Did you know him?"

"Ronnie Garrett. He's been around a while. Younger than your uncle—he's only in his thirties, maybe your age—but he was an associate of Paulie's for a long time."

"An associate."

She sparked another cigarette. "That's what I said."

I sipped my coffee. "Do you know what happened?"

"They got shot, that's what happened." Tightening her lips, her chin held firm against the onslaught of coming tears, but she managed to chase them away before even a single drop surfaced. "Didn't the cops tell you?"

"I guess I meant why," I said quietly.

Louise released some air through her nostrils that could have been a sigh or perhaps even an attempt at ironic laughter, I couldn't be sure. Like a dated movie queen she smoked her cigarette dramatically for a while before answering as a gray cloud of smoke engulfed us. "Your uncle was in an unforgiving business, you know that."

"I never really knew *what* business he was in."

"Sure you did. Not knowing isn't the same as not wanting to know." She peered at me through the smoke like a specter. "Look, this is a tough time for all of us right now. If you think I'm going to sit here and dance with you about this bullshit then you got the wrong gal, OK? Your uncle was a lot of things, but never the monster you thought. He was what he was. Period. He missed you, never stopped talking about you. You broke his heart."

"And he broke mine."

"Not big on forgiveness, huh?"

"Depends."

"On what?"

"Maybe that's what I've been trying to get to all these years. I'm trying to understand."

"No you're not. You're trying to feel better."

"I just want to know what happened to him."

"Because he's dead now?"

I pushed my mug aside and sat back. "Because I loved him too."

Louise smashed her cigarette into the ashtray, and this time, before the tears could escape, she blotted them away with a napkin. "Paulie was a thief. What the hell did you think he was? It was his profession. I've been around criminals my whole life. My father was one, it was how I was raised, get it? I'm a knockaround girl, have been for years, I know the score, OK? When I met him he'd already done time. I did some way back for bad checks myself, so I didn't hold anything against him, you see what I'm saying? I thought he was just another mutt, another guy who'd be fun to run with for a while. I was still dancing back then. Men like your uncle don't take women like me seriously, and trust me, honey, vice versa. But Paulie was different. He was special." She swallowed hard and patted her eyes with the napkin again. "He was the one. My one and only, you see what I'm saying?"

"I'm sorry." I yanked another napkin free of the holder on the table and slid it over to her. "I didn't mean to upset you, that wasn't my intention."

"What is your *intention*?"

"I don't know, I—I'm sorry, I shouldn't have even bothered you." I reached for my wallet. "Let me pay for this and—"

"Paulie was a wheel man."

I returned my hands to the table, listened.

"He was a professional, had a lot of skills in the life, but that was his specialty—he was a driver."

"The only time I remember him being arrested was right after the summer of 1979," I said. "It had been a terrible summer." I hesitated to see if she'd bite. She didn't, but I wasn't sure if it was due to a lack of knowledge regarding the things that took place that summer or a lack of willingness to let me know she possessed it. "That fall he was arrested, and he went to prison the following year for robbery. He was in jail for the holidays, I remember that, and how upset my mother was. She kept saying it wasn't right for him to be away from us during the holidays. She couldn't see beyond his not being there, as to *why* he wasn't. Uncle and I weren't speaking at that point, but I followed what was happening in the newspapers. He was the getaway driver on some botched bank job. The rest of the crew got twenty-plus sentences but Uncle got seven-to-ten because he was only the driver, he didn't pull a gun on anyone."

"That was long before I met him, but I know he

79

did eight of the ten in maximum stir," Louise said. "He did his time like a man, but it haunted him for the rest of his life. He had nightmares, never slept real good, your uncle. Always blamed it on his time in the joint."

Among other things, I thought.

"He did straight time for a while," she said a moment later. "He tried, God knows he did, but it's a way of life for guys like Paulie, they don't know anything else. He held jobs but never for long. He was always working an angle, always looking for a score that could get us the hell out of here. When I stopped dancing and started hostessing I lost a lot of money every week. But he always made it right. He always took care of us one way or another. I didn't ask about specifics — and he never told me — because that puts you in danger. If you know things, you're responsible for them; you see what I mean? So he always kept me far enough out of it so I didn't know exactly what he was doing. It was better that way."

Fifty-six years old and still trying to work the angles, I thought. It seemed incomprehensible that Uncle could have been pushing sixty, much less still a criminal at that age. While most men in their late fifties had settled down he'd still been swimming upstream, bucking the system and making his own rules.

"He was on the same small crew for a long time," Louise said. "Same guys, for the most part. Guys he knew and trusted. Him, Ronnie Garrett, Joey Peluso and Walt Dunham. Right before this job Walt Dunham got arrested, there was a warrant out on him for an A&B—assault and battery—on some guy at a bar. Anyways, Walt never made the trip. He's still sitting in county waiting on a trial because of all his priors for violent offenses. All I know is, Paulie and the other two pulled a job that had to do with some jewelry. Maybe a store, maybe a courier, I don't know. It was an out of town caper, I know that much. Paulie packed a small bag, enough for a couple days, mostly summer clothes so it must've been somewhere warm. California, Florida— whatever. How they got the lead I don't know. But a job this big, where the swag was so valuable isn't something pros like Paulie and his crew would've done locally—the job would've been too dangerous to pull in their own backyard and the merchandise too hot. Anyway, he was gone for three days. When he came back he was nervous, and that wasn't like him, but he said everything was OK, that everything went fine. Obviously it didn't."

"Obviously," I muttered.

"Two days later he was dead." The words fell from her mouth as if she were unaware of them.

"So this Dunham guy's in jail even before they do the job, and Ronnie Garrett and Uncle end up dead two days after they get back. What about the other guy? Peluso."

"What about him?"

"Where is he?"

"He's around. Covering his tracks, I'm sure. It's no secret they were partners so it's only a matter of time before the cops haul his ass in for questioning. He won't run. Not yet. Running makes you look guilty. If he knows they got nothing on him he'll just bide his time, eventually this'll all blow over. Then he'll go. One day, he'll just go. The cops will probably haul me in too, but I don't know anything, and what little I do know I won't be telling those bastards. Just going through the motions for me."

I leaned closer across the table. "So this Peluso character killed Uncle and Garrett?"

"Who knows?"

"But you said they worked together for years, that Uncle trusted him. Why would—"

"Because it was a lot of money. Isn't it always love or money? I don't know how much, but I know Paulie said it'd be enough for us to get out of here once and for all. He was talking about going to Italy. He always wanted to see it but we never had enough cash. He said if this worked out we could live there if we wanted. If he was serious then that's the kind of money even an old friend might kill you for. At the end of the day they're all criminals. You have to remember that. You swim with sharks sooner or later somebody gets bit."

"Do you know where I can find this guy?"

"Peluso?" Louise released a loud and bawdy laugh I hadn't expected, one so incompatible with her appearance it was unsettling. A single burst that left her as quickly as she'd summoned it, with a shake of her head she said, "Are you out of your mind? You think you can show up on his doorstep and start asking questions like you're asking me? Aren't you a schoolteacher? You're just a bit out of your league." This time she leaned closer, across the table. "These kind of people, they'll kill you, understand? You want your mother to have to bury her son and her brother all in one week? You help us bury your uncle and put him to rest. Then you go back up north and you get on with your little life and you forget about all this. You have a wife up there, don't you?"

Martha and I had been married in Maine in a small, quiet and private ceremony nearly ten years before, which meant that it had been right around the time he and Louise had started seeing each other. "Yes."

"Then do what you have to do here and go home to her."

"This isn't about her," I said. "It's about Uncle."

"No it's not. It's about you. You got your memories of Paulie—good and bad—live with them." She gazed out the window at the snowflakes as a renegade tear crept across her cheek to her jaw line and dangled there like a raindrop. "It's all any of us can do."

* * *

After Boone and I split up I headed back home. The front light was on, as was the one over the sink in the kitchen, so I knew that at some point my mother had come downstairs and turned them on for me. But she had long since gone back to bed. The house was silent. I found my way upstairs and collapsed into bed, but sleep refused to come and I was up all night staring at patterns on the ceiling and watching my thoughts and fears convert to endless loops of film in my mind.

Hours later I sat on the windowsill in my bedroom and watched the sun rise. As it took its place in the sky, glowing over the nearby ocean and shining down on our world, perhaps fittingly, it reminded me of a doting mother hovering over her children. For some reason I thought of my father for the first time in a long while. Visions of him in his wrinkled suits haunted me, and I wondered if he ever thought of me, of any of us. But such concepts seemed traitorous somehow, so I let them go. They faded quickly.

Gone, just like him.

Not long after sunrise I heard Angela and our mother begin to stir.

When my door opened a few moments later, I saw my mother standing there barefoot and wearing a lightweight bathrobe. Her hair was mussed and her face looked pale without makeup, drawn. An entire conversation passed between us without either of us uttering a word. The sound of tires on the gravel driveway outside distracted me, and I looked back out the window. Uncle's Camaro was idling there, and I could just make him out, sitting behind the wheel, sunglasses concealing his eyes and a cigarette dangling from his mouth.

"Uncle and I have to take Angie to the doctor. We'll be back in a bit."

I nodded.

"Have you been to bed, Andy?"

"Not really." I heard her feet padding across the

floor as she approached me.

"Try to get some sleep, honey," she said, her warm hands rubbing my back. "Everything's going to be all right. Angie's OK, we just want to be sure."

I left the window, walked over to my bed and sat down. I knew what was coming.

"Look," she said, following and crouching next to me. Her eyes were heavy and sleepy. "This is hard for all of us, but we had to make some decisions about what happened to your sister. Very difficult decisions, do you understand?"

"I guess."

"We're going to keep this in the family, Andy. Your uncle knows a doctor who can be discreet about this. Angie's only twelve, there's no reason for this to get out."

"You make it sound like she did something wrong."

She shook her head as if prepared to better explain herself then seemed to realize my point. "It stays in the family," she said sternly. "End of discussion."

"OK."

Softening a bit, she touched my knee and tried her best to smile. "I need you to be strong right now, Andy. I need you to be a man. We have to stick together now more than ever, OK? We have to look out for each other. None of this leaves the family. No one is to know about any of this. Not even Boone. *No one.* We just go on and we put it behind us, OK? If we need to talk about it, we do it with each other. I'm always here for you, you know that, and so is Uncle. But no one else is to know about this, and I mean it, Andy. Promise me. I need your word."

"What about Michael Ring? *He* knows."

She stiffened again, the mention of his name causing her physical appearance to shift. Pushing herself back to her feet with a muffled sigh she said, "Never mind about him."

"Aren't you going to tell the police? You can't let him get away with what he did."

"He'll get what's coming to him." Her jaw clenched and I could see it working along the side of her mouth as she tried to contain her rage. "People like that always do."

"What if he does?" I goaded. "Do we keep *that* in the family too?"

I tried to read her expression, curious as to whether Uncle had told her about my refusing to fight. In the end, it hardly mattered.

My mother moved away, creating a chasm between us we were never again fully able to fuse. The distance established that morning by her seemingly simple act of walking a few steps away became a gulf that remained between us from that point forward, a hollow place void not of love or affection, but of camaraderie, solidarity, understanding, and ultimately, respect.

She stood in my bedroom doorway with her back to me. "Will you promise me? Will you give me your word, Andy?"

"Yes," I said. "I give you my word."

Uncle waited in the car until Angela and my

mother joined him there. I watched the car drive off, taking with it more than just members of my family. The entire world and nearly everyone in it I cared for vanished at the top of the street and crossed over into some other place that day. A place I believed then I could never accompany them to. Things had changed. Perceptions had become distorted, realities altered.

And there wasn't a damn thing I could do about it.

9

I walked Louise back to the *Blue Slipper* in silence. The snow fell around us just as silently, blanketing the otherwise grimy neighborhood in temporary splendor, a hoax to deceive us into believing we were somewhere magnificent. As we closed on the club the barely audible thumping music from within bled free. Louise hesitated at the front doors then turned to me, her expression set as if to say something of great importance. But in the end she said nothing, and we both stood there a while in a sea of white flakes and visible breath.

"Guess I'll see you tonight over at your mother's," she said.

I impulsively reached over, put my arms around her and hugged her gently. I was probably even more surprised by this than she was, but despite the awkwardness it seemed appropriate under the circumstances. The smell of her perfume was more invasive up close, and her body felt cold, unexpectedly frail and artificial, nearly mannequin-like.

"For what it's worth," I whispered, "I'm sorry." Her arms briefly found my shoulders, but she remained rigid, so I let her go and stepped back.

The corner of her mouth curled with such subtlety I couldn't be sure if it was a smile or a sneer, and without a word she disappeared through the front doors of the club.

As I walked across the lot I noticed a phone booth across the street. I crossed quickly, my feet sloshing in the newly formed puddles of slush. Hanging from a shelf in the booth by a thick metal cord was a tattered phonebook. I flipped through it, located the name and address I was looking for then headed back to my car.

I drove for nearly ten minutes, following a winding road that alternated between occasional ramshackle cottages littered along more rural stretches and brief clusters of independent commercial property leftover from an era prior to the expansive growth of downtown Warden. The address I was searching for was near the literal outskirts of town. At a small intersection I pulled over into the snow-covered dirt lot of a liquor store that had been there since I was a child. Across from it sat a lumberyard. A bar and grill occupied one remaining corner, a hardware store the other.

A neon beer sign in the liquor store window distracted me. An elderly couple named McMullen had owned the store in my youth, but they had died years ago and the establishment had since been renamed Warden Liquor.

Along the side of the package store an old

wooden staircase lead to the lone apartment above it. When I was a kid an older man and hapless alcoholic named Wiley had lived there. Wiry, with stringy gray hair, he wore combat fatigues and rode a rickety bicycle around town from bar to bar every day, and I remembered him not because he had often been the brunt of jokes, but because even then I had found him fascinating. Always alone and always drunk, my mother had once told me he was a veteran of World War II who had lost his mind during combat and that despite his problems he was to be respected. I'd always wondered what the full story behind Wiley was but never had the nerve to ask, so to me, and I suspect most everyone else, he was destined to forever remain an enigma.

Black numbers to the left of the liquor store's front door read: 23. I followed the edge of the building upward, along the staircase to the door at the top, where another set of numbers read: 23 1/2. Nothing much had changed here. Although we rarely ventured to this far end of town, to the best of my recollection the building looked the same as it had in my youth. Only now, all these years later, Wiley was long dead and buried, his agony and demons mere memories of people like me, people who never even knew him. And ironically, at least according to the phonebook, this tiny apartment above the liquor store was now the home of Desmond Boone.

* * *

Three days came and went without incident, as far as I knew.

My mother took some time off from work to look after Angela, and I suppose, in the hopes of collecting herself as well. Our house assumed an otherworldly feel, like a monastery where the inhabitants had taken vows of silence and above which hung a perpetual sense of mysticism and cloistered segregation from the outside world. Although we were Roman Catholic by birth, prior to the events that summer I would not have considered our family particularly religious or our home exceptionally spiritual, but there was an undeniable presence of the divine about us in those days following Angela's attack. I could sense it in the air, its essence, a feeling that something else was with us, something ubiquitous but normally unrecognized now revealed. And yet I felt no real connection to it, like it was in our midst but independent of us. A watcher, perhaps, a sentinel of sorts, watching over us from some other place; wanting us to listen but unable to force us to do so. For the most part we moved about and interacted like strangers sharing a boardinghouse, carefully and quietly going through the motions of everyday life, such as it was.

Angela gradually began to emerge from her previous state, and she and I would spend a few minutes each morning at the kitchen table. Our normal raucous behavior and laughter-filled conversations were no more, replaced instead with uncomfortable stillness. On those rare occasions when we did speak, it was by rote and never concerned what had happened. Angela was gone even when she was sitting right next to me, hidden in thoughts no one else could share.

On one afternoon I went to her room to find her sitting at the foot of her bed surrounded by her stuffed animals. She had positioned them about her in uniform circular walls so that they faced her, their glass eyes watching over her, their stitched limbs outstretched to protect her. Sitting cross-legged in the center, she cradled her favorite doll in her arms, her head cocked and her chin resting on her shoulder, small lips moving silently as she whispered to her. Angela looked up when I crossed the doorway, and I thought for a moment she might smile. But she blinked at me with her beautiful eyes, slow and purposeful blinks that let me know she was as close to all right as she was likely to get in the next few days, then resumed her conversation with the doll. In her own pain, confusion, fear and anger, she had found refuge and solace in consoling a baby not of flesh, blood and bone, but plastic. In the moment, it made perfect sense, and summoned up exactly who Angela was in a way she could've never expressed verbally. I had never before wanted to hold my sister so badly. I entered the room, leaned over and kissed the top of her head the way Uncle often did.

After a moment I moved to a rocking chair in the corner of the room and sat down. I never interrupted her or spoke a word, only sat watching over her, being with her, near her, and for the first time was able to do so without seeing the horrible visions in my mind. Each time I had thought of her, looked at her, or even heard her moving about the house prior to that, I had guiltily coupled her with the savagery she had endured. For me, they had become one in the same, and it wasn't until that otherwise innocuous moment that I was able to separate her face, her tiny body, her movements and sounds from what had happened to her, from what had been perpetrated against her, and with that newfound revelation, rediscovered the ability to once again see my sister—and only my sister—as I had previously. It was only Angie, only me, and short-lived as that instant may or may not have been, for the time being, we were all right again.

Perhaps motivated by this epiphany, or perhaps an extension of it, the hallowed presence I had felt in our house grew stronger, a presence of love and warmth and acceptance and hope that pushed away all the darkness, if only for a little while. It was pleased, and for those few hours that afternoon, so were we.

When I left Angela's room the warmth dissipated, and I found myself swallowed again by the outside world. I spent the rest of the day at the picnic table in the backyard, staring at a blank sheet of paper loaded into my typewriter. Meaningful words in any form refused to come, as if I were sleepwalking and only vaguely aware of my own existence.

My mother spent most of her time drinking and sitting in the den staring at the walls. She rarely showered or dressed until late in the afternoon, then prepared simple meals, soup or sandwiches for dinner each night, before returning to her roost in the den. Now and then she'd talk on the telephone, mostly to Uncle, who for some reason also stayed away during those three days, but the rest of the time she'd sit quietly and sip her drink. It was a habit my mother would never lose.

Over the course of those three uneventful days Boone called a few times but I never agreed to see him. I knew he'd understand that this was a time the three of us — my mother, Angela and myself — needed to be together, even if we spent that time together apart, wandering about our small house and smaller yard, filling spaces with sighs and footfalls, breath and quiet attendance, because for each of us to know the others were there was somehow enough.

On the fourth day of our self-imposed vigil, Angela and I were playing checkers at the picnic table when our mother slipped through the backdoor to let us know she was going off with Uncle for a while. I remember her face that day, because it was even more drawn and pale than usual. She had made an attempt at styling her hair but it still looked unusually mussed, and her clothes hung on her, wrinkled and thrown together with little care. She looked like she hadn't slept in a very long time, and probably hadn't.

I wondered if she felt the same benevolent presence in our home that I had, or if it was simply a figment of my imagination, wishful thoughts conjured to protect us all.

"I'm going out with Uncle for a while," she said softly. "I'll be back soon OK?"

"OK," I answered for both of us. I made my move, sliding a black checker onto a new square. When I looked up to say goodbye, she was already gone. The screen door slapped the frame then came to rest in her wake. I noticed Angela staring after her.

"Angie?"

She turned at me.

"Your move."

On the fifth day, just when I'd started to think that perhaps everything would be all right, everything changed yet again. All I had thought healed became further diseased, and everything I feared the most became reality.

10

The world is not the same when it snows. Things look differently, feel differently, and even sounds — natural and otherwise — become altered. The same can be said of silences, as there is nothing quite like the hush that accompanies a snow-covered landscape. Coupled with the steady swirl of flakes, it reminded me of the obvious — or what should have been obvious — that I was alive. I often felt like I was under a spell that left me largely unaware, a machine on automatic pilot. But in that silence and snow, breathing fresh air and standing beneath the immensity of a gray and vacant sky, it all slipped away.

As I hesitated at the top of the staircase alongside the liquor store, I looked out over the woods in the distance. Amidst the otherwise innate beauty of such a setting, between the back lot and a sea of trees draped in white, the rotted carcass of an old automobile sat alone on a stretch of flatland like a work of modern art, offering a fitting, if not perverse dichotomy.

Nothing moved but the falling snow.

I knocked on the door and after several moments heard sounds of movement within the apartment. "Yeah?" a gruff voice asked.

"Boone?"

"Who's there?"

I leaned closer; spoke to the door. "It's Andy."

"Who?"

"Boone, it's Andy DeMarco."

A deadbolt clicked free and the door pulled open with an abrupt scraping sound. There was not much light in the apartment behind him so it took me a moment to make out the person in the doorway. I had not seen Desmond Boone in more than ten years but it appeared as if he'd aged twenty in that time. He squinted at the intrusive light, his face contorted. He was either hung over or had just woken up. Maybe both.

"Boone," I said through a smile. "It's good to see you."

He stared at me a moment as if he were trying to place me. Still quite heavy, he was dressed in an old sweatshirt and sweat pants and looked slovenly as ever. His once unruly bush of red hair was only a memory, as he had gone almost completely bald, and his face was bloated, pale, unhealthy looking.

"Boone? You all right?"

This time he responded with an awkward nod and self-consciously wiped his hands on his shirt. "Andy," he finally said. "Holy shit, I—I didn't expect to see you standing here. Figured it was a bill collector or some douche bag selling something."

"I'm back in town for a couple days, needed to see you."

"Yeah," he mumbled. "I heard about—I was real sorry to hear about your uncle."

"Me too." I shrugged snow from my coat. "Can I come in or is this a bad time?"

Boone seemed to ponder my question with more intensity than it warranted. "Um, yeah—sure, it's kind of messy in here, I didn't get a chance to clean up yet this week, but—yeah, of course, man, come on in."

The interior of the apartment was dark, musty and cluttered. An array of smells hit me, an odd fusion of stale foods, stagnant air and body odor that was so strong I had to fight the urge to bring a hand to my face to cover my nose and mouth.

In some ways I felt like I'd entered a sacred haven and solved a mystery of our childhood simply by entering the apartment. For so many years it had been known as the place where poor "crazy" Wiley had lived, and stories had circulated about what it looked like inside or what he did or didn't do within these four walls, that it had become a kind of legend, one of those places kids spoke of on Halloween or at sleepovers. Wiley had been accused of everything from collecting bodies in the apartment to doing odd experiments on unsuspecting children he kidnapped—all foolishness, of course, but the kind of fodder prepubescent imaginations thrive on.

Now that I was here, it was anything but mysterious, and I couldn't help but think back to the days when Boone and I had been two kids sitting on our bicycles watching Wiley go in or out of this place, wholly unaware that fate had conspired to one day land Boone here as well. With his odd appearance, eccentric behavior and impoverished lifestyle, I wondered if kids in town these days told the same silly stories about Boone that we had once told about Wiley.

As my eyes adjusted to the sudden lack of light, I found myself in a cramped living room with low ceilings and a large, badly stained throw rug in the center of the floor. Clothes, empty pizza boxes and an assortment of spent liquor bottles were strewn from one end of the room to the next. Against one wall was a cabinet that housed a small television on one shelf and a boom box on another. Atop the cabinet were three framed photographs faded with age and blurred through a film of filth that had collected across the glass. One was of Boone with his brother and parents, a posed and overly formal looking picture reminiscent of family portraits in the 60s. Boone was quite young in the photograph, perhaps five or six, bright eyes and that memorable unruly red hair his dominant features even then. He was smiling widely, as if he'd been laughing when the photographer snapped the picture. The second was a picture of his brother Jonathan in full football regalia that captured him in the prime of his physical prowess and athletic glory. He had gone on to play at Ohio State on a football scholarship, and though he'd been an athletic god in a town like Warden, his college career turned out to be less than spectacular, and his dreams of one day playing in the NFL never came to fruition.

Last I knew he'd become a gym teacher somewhere in the Midwest.

As poignant as the first two photographs were, particularly considering the way his family had treated him over the years, the third one hit me hardest of all. Standing in his living room amidst the mess, I stared open-mouthed at the picture, remembering the night it was taken like it was only days rather than years ago.

Uncle had taken the two of us to a carnival that had passed through Warden one summer, and at one point we had stopped to have our picture taken standing behind a plasterboard front painted to look like the headless bodies of two well-sculpted bodybuilders. Those having their pictures taken would stand behind it and rest their chin on the cutaway portion, thus creating the illusion that the body and head belonged to the same person. With the bright lights of a Ferris Wheel in the night sky behind us, versions of Boone and myself—eleven-year-old versions—stared back at me from a place and time generally reserved for the foggy landscape of dreams and distant memory.

"Sorry about the mess, man, I really need to clean this place up." Boone swept by me, gathering dirty laundry from the couch. "Have a—have a seat."

I did, sitting carefully on the edge of the sofa as he lumbered into a small hallway between the room we were in and a tiny kitchenette on the other side of the apartment. The sink was overflowing with dishes covered in grime, and the kitchen table was piled high with mail and old newspapers. But for an old Rolling Stones poster and a centerfold featuring a busty brunette from *Hustler* or some similar magazine, the walls in the living room were bare and painted a curious shade of bluish-gray that lent an even greater degree of dreariness to what was an already gloomy apartment.

Boone threw the pile of clothes into the hallway then returned to the living room and stood before me looking much like a child suddenly summoned to the principal's office. "Jesus," he said sheepishly, "I can't—dude, I can't believe you're sitting here."

It took me several seconds to form a response, as I wanted to apologize for having not seen him in so long, for letting our relationship lapse, but instead I smiled and shrugged and said, "How're things, Boone? You OK?"

"Yeah, I mean—well, yeah, I'm cool."

The last I had heard he worked at a fish processing plant in town, but it looked as if he hadn't left his apartment in months, much less to go to work. "Are you still working at the plant?"

"Nah, I'm ah, kind of between gigs at the moment." He stuffed his hands into the pockets of his sweat pants and shuffled about awkwardly, favoring his right leg. "Being the graceful motherfucker I am, I fell down the stairs a couple months ago and busted up my knee pretty bad. Bit of advice, dancing down a staircase after drinking a fifth of vodka is never as good an idea as it seems at the time."

Glimpsing his former humor, I laughed lightly, but it was more a courtesy than a genuine reaction. There no longer seemed to be anything funny about Desmond Boone.

"I had a couple operations on it and had to do all this therapy shit, but the doctors told me it wouldn't ever be like it was before. So anyway, I'm on disability for now. Sucks, it's not much — I'm trying to live on a month what I used to live on a week — but what the hell you gonna do, right?" He hobbled over to a chair across from the couch and plopped himself onto it without bothering to brush away the debris and clothing. "How's the teaching thing working out, you still doing that?"

"Yup, still at it."

His eyes brightened a bit. "Still writing your stories?"

"Now and then," I said. "But not much anymore."

"That's too bad," he said softly. "You always wrote the coolest stories."

"Things change, I guess."

"You can say that again." He glanced away, uncertain. "I see your mom sometimes around town. She said you got married."

"Ten years ago now."

He nodded. "Long time."

"Seems like my thirties are just flying by."

"It goes quick. Too goddamn quick, you ask me."

"For sure."

"Last time I saw you I remember you saying you

were getting engaged or something." He scratched his head. "Remember when we had lunch that time?"

I did. I'd come home briefly to visit my mother and had arranged to meet Boone for lunch. We hadn't been in each other's company for a few years and while the get-together was pleasant enough it was also awkward and a bit strained. Our lives had gone in different directions, and through no fault of his own, Boone represented to me a past I wanted to forget, a connection to a time and to events I wanted to put behind me, and I was sure I represented the same to him in many ways. We shared the same secrets, and those secrets haunted us both, then and now.

I had not seen him since.

"I'm sorry it's been so long," I finally managed. "It's really good to see you."

"You too, man." He smiled, and this time it was genuine. "Can you believe I'm living in Crazy Wiley's old place?"

I hadn't planned to say anything, but since he mentioned it, I played along. "Last time I saw you, you were still living at the house."

"Yeah, well, seven years ago my dad died."

Despite my memories of the man and the cruelty he'd shown toward his son, I offered the appropriate condolences.

"Couple years later my mom got sick and I had to put her in a nursing home. That Alzheimer's is some horrible shit, man. Horrible shit. She didn't even know who I was toward the end." He stared at the floor as if recalling a specific episode. A moment later he snapped out of it with a helpless shrug. "They took everything to pay for her care — even her house — can you believe that? Her and my father worked their whole lives. She gets sick before her time and has to go into a nursing home and those bastards took everything they worked all those years for. Me and Jonathan were supposed to get that house. Ended up getting nothing. They put me out in the street so I had to get a place and this was about all I could afford. Jonathan didn't really give a shit, he's got his own house and the wife and kids, the whole bit, you know? He's a teacher too, Gym, though. Figures, right? *Those who can, do. Those who can't, teach. Those who can't teach, teach gym.*"

It was an old joke I'd heard before, but I laughed dutifully.

"Anyway, my mom died a couple years ago."

"I'm sorry, Boone."

"Thanks." He flashed a lonely grin. "Soon as I get this knee strong again I'll get back to work. Not sure doing what, exactly, but I've been thinking about moving. Always wanted to go to California. Heard they got more jobs out there." After another strained and uncomfortable silence Boone clapped his hands together to signal the next phase of our conversation was to begin. "Hey, you want a drink? I could use a drink."

"No thanks. I'm good."

He struggled to his feet, went to the kitchen area and retrieved a half-empty bottle of vodka from a cabinet over the sink. When he returned to his chair with the bottle and took a long pull like it was water, I realized that along with all the hard luck he'd also inherited his father's drinking problem. He held the bottle in his lap with one hand and wiped his mouth with the back of the other. "I couldn't believe it when I heard about Uncle," he said. "Couldn't believe it."

"I know the feeling."

"Couldn't believe he went out that way, not him."

I nodded but said nothing.

"I used to see him now and then around town," he said, smiling slightly. "He'd always say hi and he'd go, 'Hey Boone, how about some topless Elvis?'" What began as a laugh became a cough that emanated from deep within his lungs. "He loved it when I did that, remember?"

"Yeah," I said, matching his guarded smile with one of my own. "Who could ever forget topless Elvis?"

"That was some of my best shit." Boone took another swallow of vodka. His face darkened a bit. "So what are you doing here, man? I mean, I'm not trying to be a dick or nothing, but I haven't seen you in years, Andy. You didn't even invite me to your wedding. No phone calls, no letters, no nothing for years. Why now?"

"I'm sorry I let our friendship slip away, Boone, *truly* sorry."

"Like you said, things change, right?"

"I thought we should talk, considering the past."

"What difference does it make all these years

later? Besides, Uncle's dead."

Against my better judgment I held my hand out for the bottle. He pushed it into my palm and I took a quick gulp. The liquor spread through me like a fast moving virus, or perhaps an antidote. "I want you to go somewhere with me."

* * *

My mother and Angela were still asleep when I left the house that morning. Angela was in bed cuddled up with her stuffed animals and oblivious to my presence even when I leaned over and gently kissed her cheek. My mother's bedroom was empty, but I found her downstairs in the den, asleep in a chair. Although her chest rose and fell with the steady rhythm of sleep her features retained a look of tension and discomfort—torment—she could not escape even in a world of dreams.

I'd read the newspaper article and seen the news reports on television the evening prior, and so had they. These things rarely happened in Warden, yet my mother and Angela had pretended to be completely unaffected by what we all knew to be the truth. They were able to turn their backs on it like zombies, to say nothing and do nothing and pretend we were free of it while so many others in town came together to help.

While they slept I rode my bike to Uncle's apartment on Bay Street, a touristy part of town located near the largest beach in Warden. He lived above a bicycle shop directly across from the water that was sandwiched between a bakery and a small bookstore. Within hours the area would be mobbed with summer residents and tourists on their way to Cape Cod, but for now the neighborhood was still awakening, still suspended in serene early-morning moments, and despite its underlying commercial intent, the tranquility allowed an enchanted facade to cloak all that slept just beneath this fanciful exterior. Outsiders saw the innocence of a storybook village, but like a carny in the know, I saw the mercenary, dispassionate nature behind its colorful mask, thereby dismissing all else.

I leaned my bike against a streetlight then climbed the staircase on the side of the building.

Uncle answered my knock on his door quickly, standing just inside the entrance in a pair of boxers, his usually perfect hair mussed and looking like it needed a good washing. "Andy," he said, surprised to see me, "what are you doing here? Is everything all right?"

"No," I answered. "Nothing's all right."

He looked me over then stepped back so I could enter.

With a deep breath I walked into a modest studio apartment. But for a handful of spent beer bottles and an overflowing ashtray on a coffee table, it was neat and clean. His bed was unmade, as he had just rolled out of it, and the window shades were drawn, casting the room in near darkness. Although he had lived there for years the apartment had an institutional, impersonal aura I had always found peculiar.

Despite his fancy clothes, expensive jewelry and flashy car, Uncle had few meaningful personal possessions, and I realized years later his apartment was typical of many professional, single, lifelong criminals. It was set up and maintained with the bare essentials so that if he had to abandon it he could do so at any moment without being burdened by a living space that might in any way impede his departure. Much like him during times of intense thought or serious trouble, there was something inherently bleak about it, bleak and solitary and sad.

Uncle scratched his bare chest and switched on a small lamp. On a nightstand beside the bed was a handgun we both pretended not to see. "So what's the problem?"

"Michael Ring's missing. He's been gone for a few days. It's all over the news. *Teenage boy vanishes.* They've got search parties all over town. They're looking up in the woods and along the beaches. They even called the National Guard to check the ocean in case he went swimming and drowned." I stood glaring at him, yet I was the one who felt like a corpse twisting in the wind. I wanted so fiercely to be a man, not the kind he envisioned but enough of one to control myself, and was already failing miserably. "They're not going to find him are they?"

"Couldn't tell ya," he said.

"They're not going to find him because he's dead."

Uncle shrugged. "Never know. It's a dangerous world out there, lots of things can happen to a person. Even if he is dead, the world's not gonna stop spinning just because that piece of shit stepped off, Andy. Look, any fifteen-year-old who could attack a kid like Angie isn't worth worrying about, all right? There's no telling how many other girls he did that to, or how many he would've done it to down the road." Something in his eyes shifted, like he was remembering an old joke. "Maybe something happened to him, maybe not. Who knows? But if he's dead, so what? Who gives a shit? We know he did a lot of bad things, right? Maybe he pissed off the wrong guy."

I nodded, mostly as a means of clearing my head. "Are you the wrong guy?"

He sat on the edge of his bed. "What do you want from me, Andy?"

"The truth."

"The truth." He chuckled. "Everybody always wants the truth. Problem is nobody ever knows what the hell to do with it once they get it."

What I said in response to his dismissive laughter was not a question, and he knew it.

"You did it, didn't you."

11

Boone and I drove across town in silence, the memories gliding past distorted through a windshield smudged with ice and snow. I was certain he had searched his mind for things to say, as had I—be it small talk or things more relevant—but not a word passed between us until I pulled into the entrance to Smyth Park. I heard him shift in his seat then, saw his pudgy hands reach forward to grasp the dashboard.

"Haven't been here in a long time," he muttered.

I pulled over to the side of the dirt road, dropped the car into Park and switched off the wipers. The remainder of the pitted road leading into the park lay before us, the trees that lined either side weighted down with snow, the branches hanging to form a tunnel of white. Again, we sat quietly for a time. Watching. Thinking.

Snow fell against the windshield, slowly covered it, sealing us off.

"You never liked it here," I said.

"No." He sighed heavily. "Even all these years later it just sits here. While back some developer tried to buy it but the town blocked it. They want the park to stay the same: whole lot of nothing. History and all that."

History. They had no idea.

The last time we'd met here the things I told him—good, bad or indifferent—had shackled us together. Now I hoped they might finally set us free.

"What the hell we doing here, man?"

The car began to feel like a tomb. "Come on." I pushed open the door and was greeted by a burst of snow and a cold gust of air.

Boone pinched his face into a dramatic frown but followed me anyway.

The snow here was lighter, fluffier than the wet stuff that had been falling earlier, and but for the occasional rumble of a car along the street behind us, the quiet remained, the utter stillness. When we shuffled through the snow and moved into the stark passageway of weighted trees, Boone's breathing became labored, and the spell was broken. Still, it was like a living painting here, a space we had crossed into impossibly, two sentient creatures trekking into a beautiful but lifeless vista brushed onto canvas.

The frigid air stung my eyes, reminded me this was all real, and as we ventured into the beginnings of the park I rubbed them and focused on the open field. Boone was right. Nothing much had changed. I stuffed my hands deep into my coat pockets and hunched my shoulders up against the cold. Boone, in an inexpensive parka, looked like he was slowly freezing to death. His cheeks were bright red and his nose was running, and every few seconds he wiped it clean with the back of his sleeve then looked at me for some explanation as to what we were doing out there.

I took a few steps deeper into the park and scanned a line of trees along an incline roughly forty yards in the distance. "After the summer when everything happened," I said, my voice hollow and oddly foreign, "when Uncle ended up going to prison for that bank robbery and—"

"I remember," he said before I could finish the thought.

"We were almost sixteen by then. Things were changing."

"For you. Not so much for me."

I nodded through plumes of breath. "That year and a half or so to graduation is still a blur to me."

"You got caught up with that chick."

"Carrie Weller."

"Yeah, Carrie Weller. She still lives in town. She's a nurse's aid. Divorced, couple kids. I never liked her."

"I never liked her much either." I glanced at him and we both suppressed smiles. I hadn't thought about Carrie Weller in years. My first serious girl-friend, I remembered her mostly in severe montage; making out, having barely competent sex, arguing over the most ridiculously mundane things imagi-nable—welcome to the wonderful world of teenage romance. Time had surely weakened the power of my emotions since then, as things seldom felt that intense anymore, like they had in the days when every word and thought and action was so concentrated and passionate that it seemed we might physically implode at any moment. "Thank God it didn't last."

"Most things don't," Boone said softly.

"The things that matter do. Sometimes they falter or go off track a while, but they find their way back."

He shrugged awkwardly. "Hey those were—they were hard times, it's—I knew you were struggling with a lot of stuff."

"All I could think about was getting the hell out of this town. That's why I went to college in Rhode Island. Wasn't too far but far enough. Hell, anything outside these borders was far enough. Besides, I had to rely mostly on financial aid money, and you can't be too choosy when you're going on someone else's dime."

"At least you got to go."

"But I became somebody else, Boone." I walked a few steps away, kicked lazily at the snow. "All I did was drink and party and get into fights. Christ, I'd fight at the drop of a hat—*me*—always hated that crap and there I was throwing with anybody who looked at me funny or said anything I could even remotely construe as a challenge."

"Maybe you were trying to prove something."

"That's exactly what I was doing. I did it all through college and even a few years after that. It's why it took me so long to finally land a decent job.

Not much call for a schoolteacher who spends his off-time brawling in bars." I shook my head. "I had so much anger, most of it directed at myself, ironically. I guess I wanted to convince myself and anyone else who happened to be within arm's reach that I wasn't a coward."

I could hear Boone shifting about to my side but he said nothing.

"It all changed—I changed—when I met Martha. She saved my life, really, made me realize that who I was trying so hard to be wasn't the real me. The real me was the one I'd lost before, the one I'd been before I even knew her, the one I'd buried back here in Warden with all those memories and nightmares. She helped me get myself back, Boone. She made me whole again."

"You're a lucky guy."

"Yes," I told him. "I am."

"Me, I mostly whack it to porn." He offered a self-depreciating smirk. "Ain't life grand?"

Years before I would have laughed, but I could no longer be so sure of us. Rather, I reached out and grasped his shoulder, gave it a fond squeeze then dropped my hand back to my side as the natural quiet closed in on us again. "I know back then—before I went to college, when everything happened—I know you always thought I should've reacted differently, that—"

"Andy, for crying out loud, you're talking twenty years ago. We were kids."

"I wanted to feel anger toward Michael Ring." I nearly choked on the words. I hadn't uttered his

114

name in years, and seemed to realize this only then. "I wanted to feel that kind of violent rage everyone else had, believe me I did — and eventually I *did* feel it — but in the beginning I just felt so goddamn sad. All I could feel was sorrow, Boone. This crippling sorrow for Angela and for all of us, and this con- fusion like I was in a dream and not the real world, where no one — even myself — was who or what I thought they were."

"You don't have to explain yourself on my account, man."

I didn't have the heart to tell him it wasn't solely for him, that it was as much about me as anyone else. I wanted this to cleanse us, to release us both. The wind picked up a bit, cut right through us and continued on across the open field to the forest beyond.

"Eventually that sorrow turned to hatred," I said. "I fantasized about killing the sonofabitch myself. I killed him in my mind a thousand times. But by then he was already dead, and in some ways we'd all died right along with him."

"I never felt good about what happened," Boone said a moment later. "I had to carry this around too, remember? But I figure Michael Ring got what was coming to him. He was a piece of shit, Andy, and right or wrong he got what he fucking deserved."

"But once that happened, once that's the way it went then it wasn't about him anymore," I said. "It was about us."

"See, that's always been your problem, Andy. You think too goddamn much. You're like a machine that way, you always were. The rest of us human beings have emotions too, and we react. We do stuff we shouldn't do, we say things we shouldn't say. We screw up. We do things wrong. We do things right. And sometimes — *most* of the time — the things we do aren't either one but something in between."

"I'm no different than anyone else and never pretended to be," I snapped. "Why is it always about me being holier than thou? You always accused me of that and that's never how I really felt. It was never my intention to come off that way."

"You ever listen to yourself?" Boone shook his head; his breath forming a cloudy ring about him like the motion had dislodged it from within him just then. *"It was never my intention to come off that way.* Who the hell talks like that besides you? Everything you do, everything you say is so thought out and considered from every possible angle. But in all that thinking you're the one who misses the point, Andy. You, not anybody else."

"The things Uncle did hurt us all, Boone. It made us all the same."

"You want to think that? Fine. But I live in the real world, Andy, and in the real world things aren't pretty and they aren't perfect and sometimes people let you down. Did you ever stop to think about it from his side? I doubt it. You want to play the martyr, go ahead. It's twenty years ago, who cares?" Boone glared at me. "I bet the whole pacifist thing makes for good conversation at your little academic cocktail parties, but in the real world where the rest of us live, it don't wash. You know what happened in the real world? They shot Gandhi. They blew Martin Luther King away. They nailed Jesus to a cross. *That's* what they did in the real world."

"Who are 'they', Boone?"

"What am I supposed to say? People like me? Is that it?"

"Why am I the bad guy here?"

"You're not. You weren't then and you aren't now. Michael Ring, *he* was the bad guy, Andy. Not you. And not Uncle." For an instant he became the same young boy who had referred to him as Uncle the same as Angela and I had, a boy who had worshiped Uncle because he had been everything he'd wanted and needed so desperately in his own father but could never find there. But the young Boone slipped away and the new one stood before me in the cold, shivering while shifting his weight from his bad leg to the good. "I'm gonna ask you one more time, Andy. What are we doing out here?"

I turned to the incline at the edge of the park and the row of trees silently staring back at us. Without answering I moved in their direction.

Within moments we were standing amidst the trees, peering into the beginnings of the surrounding forest. A small building sat perhaps thirty yards in, old and decayed. It had been there since the 1940s, when Smyth Park had employed a full-time caretaker, but had been empty and unattended for decades. A squat but two-story box-like structure, its brown shingles had rotted and its roof had worn. The windows were barely intact; the glass that had filled the multiple squares in each mostly distant memories now. Miraculously it managed a guise not without hope however, and appeared still structurally sound for the most part, an odd little house alone in a forest clearing, woefully awaiting the return of the man who had lived there so long ago. Or perhaps it was awaiting something else, something similar to what I had been waiting for all these years.

"The old caretaker's place," I said softly, so as not to disturb the spirits that surely slept here.

Boone struggled through the deep snow until he was alongside me. Again out of breath, he took a moment to compose himself then said, "We came out here so you could show me this?" His voice slipped between trees hundreds of years old, trees blanketed in snow and shrouded like icy ancient brides behind thick white veils. The sound escaped the clearing somewhere on the far side of the weathered building, absorbed into the past with all else that had passed through before it.

"That's where Uncle did it." I listened to the words echo through the forest, unsure if they had come from me or if the old house had whispered its secrets so only we might hear. "That's where he killed Michael Ring."

* * *

"What do you think I am," Uncle asked, slowly rising to his feet, "a dog on a leash? You think I only bite when you want me to, when it suits your needs?

118

Is that what you think? When the hell are you gonna grow up and stop being such a candy ass, Andy?" He closed the already limited gap between us and stood so close I could feel his breath against my face. "Get a clue as to how life works."

"I learned how life works from you," I said quietly.

"Don't blame me for your rose-colored view of the world," he said. "Who the hell did you think I was?"

It was a good question, and one I still didn't have the answer to.

"You think Michael Ring attacked other girls?" I asked.

He moved away, grabbed his cigarettes from the nightstand and lit one. He had a tuft of hair that fanned out across his chest and trickled down in a thin line to his navel, where it encircled it then continued on behind the front of his boxer shorts. His stomach, though flat, jiggled a bit when he walked, but the muscles in his calves and thighs and across his chest and arms were evident even when he was standing still. He didn't possess the tumor-like physique of a bodybuilder but had instead a thick, powerful look to his body. He seemed someone else entirely out of clothes, and ironically less vulnerable, closer to some base segment of nature, perhaps, a stripped-down primordial version of that which he had allegedly evolved from. I noticed a bulging vein that ran along his bicep as he bent his arm to bring the lighter to the tip of his cigarette, but looked away once he tossed the lighter aside so he wouldn't interpret my stare as a challenge.

"Criminals have a pattern," he said. "They start young. He probably raped more little girls than we'll ever know, and you can bank on this, he would've kept doing it until somebody stopped him. They don't stop on their own. Those kind never do."

"Does that just go for rapists?" I asked. "Or does that include killers too?"

He smoked his cigarette for a moment then looked me in the eye. "Andy, you and Angela are the closest thing I'll probably ever have to kids of my own. You're my nephew, and I love you. I'd do anything in the world for you, and anything in the world for your mother and for Angela. You're my family, and you're the whole world to me, all of you. I hope you know that." He squared his shoulders, and his face darkened. "But I am what I am, Andy. I do what I do."

I turned to the door, tears of anger already blurring my vision. "Me too."

"You gonna turn me in?" I heard him ask from behind me. "Is that what you're telling me?"

"Turn you in for what?" I asked without looking back. "You haven't admitted a thing."

"Would it make you feel better if I did? Is that what you want? You want me to explain myself, is that it? I gotta explain myself to *you* now, that how it works?"

Memories of Angela and me sitting together playing checkers blinked across my mind's eye, our mother standing near the back door telling us lies, her lips slightly out of sync with the sound of her voice echoing in my head. My heart sunk. "It was Mom, wasn't it? You did it because *she* wanted you to."

Uncle blanched, left the cigarette dangling between his lips and stepped closer to me, his movements oddly sinister. "Don't ever say shit like that about your mother. *Ever.* You hear me? You got any idea what that woman's been through for you kids, any idea at all? That's your mother, you talk about her you do it with respect."

"I heard you. I heard you talking, I heard what she said. You didn't want to do it, you told her but she—"

"She was upset, Andy. She'd just found out what happened, cut her some slack."

"She made you—"

"She didn't make me do anything." He plucked the cigarette from his mouth and held it down by his side as smoke slowly escaped his nostrils. "Leave her out of this."

I wanted to sit down but remained frozen near the door. "She's part of it too, she's—"

"We're *all* part of it," he snapped. "Now I'm not gonna tell you again, Andy. Leave your mother out of this. You came here to talk to me, right? So talk. Say your piece."

"I've got nothing else to say." I turned to leave.

"You'd side with a kid who forced himself on your sister over me? *Me?* What the hell happened to you? I never thought there was any room between you and me. I thought we were pals. I thought it was you and me like always. Buds forever." When I said nothing in response he followed me to the door. "Maybe you need to think about Angela and your mother, and what all this is going to put them through. Don't you think they've been through enough already? Or don't you care about them anymore either?"

"Is that who you're thinking about right now — Mom and Angie?" I finally found the courage to face him again. "Is that who you were thinking about when you murdered Michael Ring?"

"They won't look for him forever," he said suddenly, as if that were the point. "He ran away, or maybe something did happen to him — something bad — but remember when I told you I'd check him out? I did, and the Ring's are poor, nobody in that family's got any pull anywhere. It's not like some senator's kid's gone missing, right? In a couple weeks nobody's gonna give a shit. He'll just be one more runaway punk, that's all."

"Only he didn't run away," I said.

"You know, most guys would've just attacked that prick without even thinking about themselves or the consequences or any of that. They would've just attacked the bastard. But not you, nah, you're too good for that. You're above all that, right?" He laughed lightly, again in a dismissive way. "What's wrong with you? Why do you even care about him?"

I felt something snap inside me, something emotional rather than physical, as though some portion of my soul had burst like an internal organ. "I *don't* care about him! I don't give a shit about him! Why can't you see that?" My body was trembling so violently I could barely stand still.

Neither of us spoke for a while, and after a moment I felt myself calming and coming back under some semblance of control. "I don't care about him," I said softly. "I care about *you*. I don't want you to be this, I don't want you—"

"Always remember, Andy," he said, his laughter gone, "there's the way you want the world to be…and the way it just fucking is."

"I love you, Uncle, but—"

"I know you do." He pointed to an old chair with a defeated motion. "Sit down."

"I'm not—"

"*Sit down.*"

I turned from the door and slowly lowered myself into the chair.

Nodding slowly, as if trying to convince himself along with me, he sighed and said, "Here's what you think you want to know."

12

We stood watching the old caretaker's house, the growing winter wind sweeping through us as if we'd become translucent somehow, as exposed and vulnerable as the open field behind us. The wind filtered through the forest, collected among the clusters of trees and drew clumps of snow from their branches. Discarded new skin, it fell silently to the ground like powdery specters fleeing the carcass of one world in favor of another. And I envied them.

"How do you know?" Boone finally asked, his voice trembling.

I saw Uncle then, standing just beyond one of the few remaining windowpanes, the cracked glass splintering and distorting his face and those of the two children standing on either side of him, their hands gently held in his own. They refused to look at me, but I recognized them too. Uncle smiled the way he so often had, with his eyes first, and cocked his head slightly to the side, his shoulders gliding up then down in a subtle though apologetic shrug. The wisdom had returned to those eyes, nesting there with longing and an odd look of peace I had never before seen in them. Closer to Heaven than Hell now, he nodded slowly, knowing I would understand. Releasing me.

"Uncle brought him here," I heard myself answer. "No one was looking for him yet."

I couldn't be sure if the profound feeling of dread in the air existed because of all that had happened here or if it was just a product of my mind. Maybe ghosts and the actions of the dead left behind a residue as real as anything else, though it no longer seemed to matter. The vision of Uncle, Angela and myself standing behind fractured panes of glass slowly dissolved, leaving behind only snow and cold and memory; a distant winter dream.

Boone stumbled back a bit, no longer wanting to get too close. He looked at me helplessly. "But they — they searched these woods and they must've searched this place too, they — "

"By the time they started looking here it was long over. They had no reason to suspect anything happened here, and all they found was an old rotting building. Uncle was gone. No more evidence," I said flatly. "And no more Michael Ring."

"I don't want to be here," Boone said, his nose running and his lips shivering uncontrollably. "What the hell you bring me here for?"

I wanted to answer, but the screams from within that old house had already begun.

That morning Martha comes to me like an apparition, like just another ghost slipping through the walls, skipping across time and reason to hover in that spot where she so often does. Just beyond the foot of our bed, she stands alone, this ghost, barely visible in the soft glow of light falling from the earliest traces of a new dawn. Her hair is undone and hangs to her shoulders, straight and full and offering glimpses of natural auburn amidst the gentle brown. She wears only an old sweatshirt, one too large for her — one of mine — her hands hidden in the cuffs, the curves of her body concealed until the bottom of the shirt ends at the midpoint of her thighs. I notice the smooth skin there; follow it to her shins and bare feet, and when I return my sleepy gaze to her face she smiles at me with a subtle turn of her lips and a sparkle in her eyes.

At the very foot of the bed, the two kittens are snuggled together as if holding onto each other for dear life, which perhaps they are, asleep on a tiny blanket of their own.

The phone rings but Martha doesn't seem to hear it, and in the near dark, lying on my side among a tangle of sheets and blankets and comforter, I can only guess where the dream ends and certainty begins.

Flashes of an old chair and a blurred form tied to it, hands and feet bound, a bloodied face, eyes wide with terror, a mouth covered with duct tape and the grunts and pleas muffled beneath it bled from deep within the old caretaker's house, stained the snow in sprays and spatters like crimson rain. The falling flakes quickly covered the past, a fresh blanket thrown over a rotting corpse.

Uncle stared at me through the windows, a gun in his hand. In the shadows behind him was someone else. I squinted at the forest as if to better see whom it was, but had solved these mysteries years before. Like so much of my life prior to Uncle's death, maybe this too was just for show. Maybe what really existed behind the dark curtains in my mind were things I had not allowed myself to see until I knew for sure that he was dead and gone, because only then could I somehow even hope to make sense of them.

Boone staggered about somewhere nearby, furiously crushing snow with his heavy footfalls. "No reason for us to be here," he said, the emotion coupling with the bitter cold causing his voice to crack. "No reason."

I closed my eyes and tilted my head back; let the snowflakes tickle my face. But even in the dark— perhaps especially in the dark—the shadows behind Uncle parted and I could see Michael Ring, his long hair hanging like string, matted with dark red splotches that clung to it like thick perspiration, his face a mass of blood and tears, nose leaking equal parts blood and snot as he struggled to breathe through his nostrils, cheeks puffing, mouth hidden behind tape, eyes swollen and beaten and filled with terror. He made a kind of odd howling sound that emanated from deep within him, from some dark, lonely, primeval place. The front of his shirt was covered in blood and stuck to him like a second skin, and the lap of his pants was covered with a dark circular stain that made a path down one of his legs to a small puddle on the floor below.

When I opened my eyes the light temporarily blinded me, but even through the flash I could see my mother there now too, standing near the door to the old house, huddled there like a child awakened by nightmares but suddenly aware that escaping sleep had not been enough, because the monsters had followed her.

Martha stares at me, hands still hidden in the cuffs of the sweatshirt but folded one atop the other. I know now that she has heard the phone ringing, but she makes no move to answer it, and at first, neither do I.

"No one calls at this hour with good news," she says sadly.

I nod and look to her for help, for an avenue of escape. But there is none, and we both know it.

As Martha watches I place the phone to my ear and in a sleepy voice say, "Yes?"

"Mr. DeMarco?" a voice asks.

"Yes."

"Mr. Andrew DeMarco?"

"Yes."

He stood next to the chair, the gun held down against his thigh. My mother, still by the door, nodded to him, her face a failed attempt at stern indifference. "Don't," she said, her voice lifting and flying through the trees.

Uncle didn't look quite human to me. He looked like he'd been replaced by some synthetic version of himself — a wax double, perhaps — cold and lifeless

128

and without joy or thought or even malice—inanimate—neither dead nor alive.

"We can't let him go," he said flatly. "Not now."

"Paulie—"

"I told you to be sure." His eyes were open but without sight. "Wait for me outside."

The boy in the chair began to struggle, his cries deadened by the duct tape covering his bloody mouth.

"Paulie, I—"

"I'll drive you home. Then I'll come back and take care of the rest," Uncle said. "But right now, go outside."

"Don't—"

"Wait for me outside, Marie." I saw him raise the gun, point it at Michael Ring's head without even looking at him. "Now. Do it now."

I replace the phone to its cradle while Martha and I gawk at it as if it's some alien instrument, something we're in awe of and from which we hope to glean great knowledge or assistance. But it grants us neither.

From the foot of the bed the sleeping kittens purr, the quiet rhythm the most peaceful and wonderful sound I have ever heard. I look at them for what seems a long time, and in their tiny bodies and infant faces sense the presence of God in a way I have not experienced since I was a young child myself. For me, Heaven seems a distance beyond comprehension, but to babies it is infinitely closer, a distance not so very far after all. I try to remember what life felt like when it was still new and anything was possible, but it too remains well beyond my reach. Somehow, I understand this is how it has to be, at least for now, and for a brief moment it all makes perfect sense.

As that flash of clarity passes, Martha steps closer and cocks her head like a baffled puppy. "Tell me," she whispers.

My mother moved along the small path between the caretaker's house and the edge of the forest, but I could not see her face. Her head was bowed and her movements were oddly smooth and dreamlike, more gliding than walking.

No longer cognizant of the cold, I trudged closer to the old building, closer to the shattered windows.

Through cobwebs separating the past from the present, I saw Uncle place the gun against Michael Ring's temple. The boy's eyes shifted, slid to the side, watched Uncle, and an odd quiet overtook him. He stopped struggling, no longer attempted speech.

In the face of the gunman I saw memories of a man laughing and playing, chasing Angela and me in our backyard, tickling us or holding us quietly on his lap, loving us and protecting us and being everything we needed him to be. I saw him dancing with our mother, twirling her around the kitchen and all of us laughing. I saw him walking with me when I still only came up to his waist, his arm draped over my small shoulders and mine wrapped around his lower back, him listening more than talking, *hearing* me, and the feel of his body, warm and strong and how it made me feel invincible and safe alongside him. I remembered all the times I had silently wished he was my father, and how later, I came to realize that in many ways, that's exactly what he was.

His voice, in a tone I had never before heard, still echoed through the decaying walls of that old house.

"*Fuck you. Fuck you* for what you did. And *fuck you* for making me do this."

The blast in my mind was deafening.

A flock of sparrows nesting in the trees overhead were spooked into sudden flight. They flew in perfect unison, looking like a single dark cloud as they whirled in one direction, swooped a bit then whirled back the opposite way before disappearing into the winter sky.

I turned away from it all. Boone was glaring at me from just beyond the tree line. "No reason for us to be here," he said again, shivering so badly now it was difficult to discern what he was saying. "Why here? Why don't you take me out to the woods behind your old house? Why not go there? Why is this place such a fucking shrine? Why don't we go out to that path where the bastard raped Angie? Why don't we go there and get all misty-eyed, you hypocritical motherfucker!"

In many ways, Boone was right. But what he didn't realize was that as he screamed at me the visions continued, visions that had always been there but I had never allowed myself to see. Uncle, holding the body down with one hand while using a saw with the other, his face spattered with blood and stray chunks of meat as the serrated teeth sliced deep through the flesh and eventually found bone. Me standing next to the corpse, kicking it, kicking what was left of Michael Ring's head again and again until all that remained was a bloody pulp. And later, Uncle carrying pieces of human being stuffed into large plastic garbage bags—the kind I had used countless times to fill with leaves after raking—to the trunk of his car, thrown there like the garbage it had become. In the visions I am there, rather than only hearing what happened from Uncle's own lips, the two of us standing there in his dingy little apartment like mannequins packed away with our secrets and lies in some dark closet. In the vision I'm able to do to Michael Ring what I had fantasized about doing for so long—to desecrate him even after death, to kick and pummel him while Uncle dismembered his body like the carcass of a recently slaughtered farm animal in order to dispose of it in the manner men like Uncle disposed of bodies. Unlike reality, where Uncle explained what had really happened in those woods the day Angela and I played checkers in our backyard, leaving me to decide what I could live with and what I could not.

Now Boone had heard the truth too, this time from my lips, and I could only hope it might finally begin to free him from this.

But here, in the snow and cold, with those dark curtains finally pulled aside, all that remained in that terrible place were the spirits of Uncle and Michael Ring. And just as I could never go to the path in the woods where Angela had been assaulted, just as I could never face that because I had no right, because it was hers to exorcise of its power and not mine, I no longer belonged in this forest either. Perhaps I never had.

I hadn't died here. They had.

* * *

I found Boone back at the car, leaned against the passenger door, hands stuffed into his jacket pockets. "I'm sorry," he said quietly. "I didn't mean that shit I said before."

"Yes you did, and it's OK."

"Uncle was like a hero to me."

"You think he was anything less to me?"

"Yeah, well to me he always will be."

Telling him that in many ways the same held true for me seemed futile. Boone saw it in simple black and white terms and I did not. Maybe it was all in how you got through the day, slept through the night and looked yourself in the mirror in the morning without losing sight of who and what you thought you were or hoped to be. Maybe those were things so personal they could never be shared or mutually understood, even between old friends. Maybe they weren't meant to be.

"I don't care what he did that day," Boone said defiantly. "He did what he had to do."

"In his own way he was trying to protect us all," I told him. "But it made everything worse. It made things even harder."

"I still can't believe he's dead."

I remembered Uncle's eyes, lifeless, sightless; his ruptured skull covered with a towel.

"You think they'll catch the guy that killed him?"

"I don't know," I said. "It's a matter for the police, Boone."

We were quiet for a while.

"Even after you left," Boone finally said, "he was still here. Always talked to me when he saw me around town. He still gave a shit." His cheeks were flushed bright red from the cold, his eyes wet. "I always thought you did too. Kept thinking you'd come back and we'd figure this all out together, like when we were kids. I always figured sooner or later you'd be back, but...but not like this."

"I had to get out of here, Boone, but it was never about leaving you behind. I needed to go when I got the chance, and I did."

"I never blamed you for going. Only for never coming back." He wiped his nose. "We were best friends."

I stood there unable to think of anything to say. It was a bit late for more apologies.

"That's why I always loved comics," he said, rescuing me. "They got it the way things should be. Good guys and bad guys. Heroes and villains, you know?"

I nodded.

"But then you get older and you figure out there aren't any such things as heroes or villains." He turned his attention to the sky now. It had stopped snowing. "There's only people who do heroic things and people who do villainous things. But either

134

way they're still just people."

"That's all any of us are, Boone, all any of us ever were. Even Uncle."

"You know I still have them?" He shrugged sadly. "My comic books, I mean."

"They must be worth a fortune by now."

"I'm gonna sell every last one of them first chance I get. Buy a plane ticket and go to California. Start all over again, you know? Maybe do it right this time."

I smiled at him. "Can I come visit?"

"Call first."

We both laughed — hard — and despite how inappropriate it may have been, despite the blood and secrets that still remained, and always would, it was exactly what we needed.

Boone grinned mischievously like he'd done so often years before, his way of letting me know he'd be all right. And I believed him. Maybe because I wanted to so desperately, maybe because he was telling the truth, I couldn't be sure which.

"Come on," I said, "I'll drive you back."

* * *

I rose slowly from the chair. Uncle's apartment and everything beyond was deathly quiet, like the world had stopped on our behalf and was awaiting a signal before it resumed.

His story finished, Uncle squinted at me through trails of cigarette smoke, and for the first time I no longer saw wisdom in his eyes, but fear.

"Grampy was a mason, right?" I asked.

After what he'd just told me, the question seemed to catch him off guard, but he answered it anyway. "Yeah. Busted his ass for years. Too bad he died when you were so little, you would've liked the old man."

"And Grammy never worked?"

"She took care of your mother and me. She ran the house. That's work."

"What did their parents do? For a living, I mean."

"What difference does it make?"

"You tell me."

His features darkened as my point finally sunk it. He was the anomaly, no one else. He hadn't come from a family of criminals or grown up around it without knowing anything different. He had chosen his life.

He moved away, dropped his cigarette into an ashtray on his nightstand. "You wanted the truth," he said evenly. "Now you got it, so don't make me ask you again. What are you going to do?"

"I'm going to be man," I told him. "Just like my uncle taught me."

13

It was not quite dark, but it was coming, closing quickly.

Boone and I hugged each other awkwardly, like the long lost friends we'd been and would soon become again. "I told you I'd never rat. I never did and I never will," he said. "None of it matters now anyway. It's over, all of it. Right, Andy? Right?"

I let him go, searched that sad face. "Right."

"Take care of yourself, OK?"

"You too. Keep in touch."

He nodded, if only to placate me. "Sure, man. Definitely."

I left Boone at the base of his steps, a lonely and disheveled man slogging toward middle age with something less than grace waving goodbye in the rearview mirror, shrinking into the whiteout as I pulled away. Though equal parts happy and sorrowful, I was glad we'd finally had our moment after all these years, but even after I'd lost sight of him I kept checking, hoping he might materialize one more time, as even then, I knew I'd probably never see Desmond Boone again.

I drove back through Warden, the temperature dropping as I went, turning the deep layers of snow to ice. The wind picked up, rattled the car with intermittent bursts. The snowstorm was over and a deep freeze was setting in, laminating and glossing over the beauty like a sealant, locking everything down. Even in areas used to such conditions, the cold tended to keep people indoors, the streets relatively empty and traffic to a minimum, and the further I puttered along the snow-covered icy roads the more it began to feel as if I were the last person in a town long deserted. Only the lights had stayed behind it seemed, flipped on in anticipation of the coming darkness, gliding along reflective sheets of ice, peeking at me from gas stations or eateries or convenience stores with each squeaking pass of the windshield wipers.

One of those lights distracted me, a small blinking neon sign advertising a bar. I pulled over, parked out front and looked the building over: A squat two-story with living quarters on the second floor and a small bar on the first. Faded curtains filled the two tiny windows facing the street, and the initial sign that had caught my attention blinked just above the front door.

Exactly the kind of place I was looking for. A pit. A place no one cared about where you could go and have a quick drink in the dark and no one bothered you unless you were looking for trouble, in which case the regular patrons would likely be happy to oblige.

After tossing my hat onto the seat I left the car, sprinted across the sidewalk and entered the bar quickly, escaping the bitter cold for a gush of forced heat and the dimly lit recess of the barroom.

It was exactly what I'd expected: A small scarred bar along the back wall, the backlight reflecting off the mirrored section of wall behind it, a few tables scattered about in the dark, a jukebox, two grizzled regulars propped against the bar, an old phone booth in one corner and a heavyset bald bartender with a rag draped over his shoulder who looked like something out of central casting.

An old Hank Williams tune played softly from the jukebox, and no one other than the bartender seemed to notice my arrival. He threw a noncommittal glance my way then returned his attention to one of the men at the bar who was droning on about something I couldn't quite make out.

I strode across the room and slid onto a stool at the bar. One of the men already there was elderly and had the cracked and weathered complexion of a man who had spent the better part of his life outdoors. He held a glass of amber liquor in his liver-spotted hands, eyes closed and head swaying slowly to the beat of the jukebox. The other was a pencil thin man in his fifties dressed in neatly pressed chinos and a sweater that hung on him like laundry on a line. His thinning hair, dyed an inky black, was combed straight back from his forehead and plastered down with something akin to axle grease, and he wore small tinted prescription glasses that sat low on his long nose. He cocked his head at me then finished what was left of his drink with a single gulp and motioned to the bartender. "One more vodka for the road, Benny," he said, slapping the glass to the counter.

The bartender grabbed a bottle of Gordon's and poured while looking at me. "What can I get you, buddy?"

"Cutty on the rocks, please."

He slid a napkin in front of me, quickly refilled a small bowl on the counter with peanuts then gave me my drink. "Haven't seen you in here before," he said through a hint of a smile.

"Just passing through."

The bartender nodded, apparently finding my response acceptable. He opened his mouth to continue the conversation when the old man at the end of the bar interrupted. "Benny," he said in a gravelly voice, "play it one more time for an old man, willya?"

The bartender chuckled, grabbed some change from the register behind him and went to the jukebox. Within seconds the same song was playing.

I sipped my drink, felt it warm my throat and beyond.

"It's good to drink," the man next to me said. "Don't you think?"

I smiled and nodded.

"Especially in the dead of winter," he answered himself. "Nothing like it. Relaxes you, right? Makes you feel better even if you got no right to feel any better. Helps you forget about all the bad for a

140

while, am I right?"

The bartender returned and gave me an apologetic grin.

"Henry," the man said, thrusting a bony hand at me.

I shook his hand. It was cold. "Andy."

"Good to meet you, my man. Good to meet you."

"Same here." I took another sip of my drink.

"Married, I see."

I glanced at my left hand and the gold wedding band on my finger, then held it up, smiled and nodded.

"Me too." He sighed heavily, raised his glass and gazed at it. "It's nice to be married. Lot of guys bitch about it but I always liked it."

I looked to the bartender but he had slid down to the end of the bar and was chatting with the old man about country music.

"How long you been married?"

"Ten years," I told him.

"Good for you." He held his glass up in tribute. "Quite an accomplishment."

I touched my glass to his. "How about you?"

"Twenty-six years, three kids—all grown now, of course. You got any kids, Andy?"

"No."

"How come?"

Since he was clearly already drunk and struck me as harmless, I let the intrusiveness of his questions go. "We just never have."

"Don't you and your old lady want kids?"

"One day maybe."

"Don't wait too long," he said quietly, assuming a more reserved demeanor. "You wait too long and one day you'll wake up and realize it's too late. We always think we got all the time in the world, you know? But we don't, my man. I'm here to tell you we don't." He slammed down the remainder of his drink. "It's like with marriage, you know? Same deal. You figure it just is what it is, right? She loves you and you love her and life goes on. Then it all changes. Just like that. Cut. Fade to fucking black."

I nodded as if I understood and turned back to my drink.

He leaned closer to me and I caught the scent of cheap aftershave. "One day I come home from work, OK? I work security at Danton Industries. You know, they make the really nice replacement windows over in the industrial park? I work security there, front desk, no big thing, but steady, I been there for years. Got a nice retirement plan and everything. My wife and kids never wanted for anything, you see what I'm saying? We weren't rich but I never let my family go without. If I had to get a second job at night or whatever, that's what I did, right? One Christmas I stocked shelves at the grocery store—no lie—me and a bunch of zit-covered little teenage pukes. They all laughed at me and shit, stupid old loser stocking shelves, right? But my family had a nice Christmas that year, so I swallowed the shit to give it to them, OK? And I did it gladly, my man. Motherfucking *gladly*. Why? Because I love my family, that's why."

142

I swallowed some more scotch, wondering now if one would be enough.

"So like I say, one day I come home from work, OK? I'm a little early because I got this sinus thing going that won't quit and I feel like a steaming pile of shit." The man's beady eyes grew dark behind the tinted lenses as he angled his glass back and crunched some ice. "Know what I find? Know what I walked into, my man? My wife doing my best friend, that's what. No lie. I walk in and they're right there on the fucking couch and she's gobbling the bastard's knob like she's under water and drawing oxygen through the motherfucker."

I suppressed a nervous laugh and awkwardly mumbled, "Jesus."

He shrugged, put his glass back on the bar. "I turned around and walked right back out. I go out and I sit in my car and I try to figure out what the hell to do, you know? And after a couple minutes my best friend—Reggie was his name—he comes stumbling out of the house—my house, *my* fucking house—all doing up his pants and shit. He comes over to the car and he goes, I swear to God, he goes: 'Henry, it ain't what you think.' *It ain't what I think?*" He laughed joylessly and shook his head, his glazed eyes struggling to remain focused. "So I just drive away because I figure if I don't, I'll kill the two of them. You got to understand, me and Reggie, we go back more than twenty years. He's been my best friend all that time. Bastard stood up for me at our wedding and everything. He's godfather to two of our kids. And he's doing Dolores. Come to find out they'd been at it for a couple years. Who knew? Not me, my man, not me. Hell of a way to find out, though, let me tell you. Hell of a way to find out."

Thankfully the bartender returned. "You all set?"

I eyed my drink. There wasn't much left. "Hit me again, would you?"

"Me too," Henry said.

The bartender frowned at him. "OK, but I'm calling you a cab."

Henry waved him away. "Fine, do what you got to do."

As the bartender moved off to fix our drinks I tried not to look at Henry directly. He was in such pain and it was so obvious it seemed obscene to notice, like gawking at the carnage of a roadside car accident.

"So anyway, now I live in this little room over the pool hall down off of Main, you know the one, Tully's? They rent rooms over there. Nothing special but it's safe and clean and they got hot water and heat."

The bartender returned, set us up and moved away.

"And Dolores and Reggie, they live together now. In my fucking house. The house I paid for, that one. The two of them live there and eat off my fucking dishes and sit on my fucking furniture and fuck in my fucking bed. Nice, huh?" He grabbed his drink like a man dying of thirst and took a long gulp. It seemed to calm him a bit. "So I take my time, you know? I take my time and I think and I think and I think about what I should do. I think and I think and I figure, hell, I got to do *something*, right? I'm a man. We're men, right, Andy?" He raised his glass again. Unsure of what else to do, I clicked mine against it in agreement. "If a man don't do what he's got to do, what he's got to do to still be a man, to still feel like a man, then something dies in you, you know what I'm saying? Something dies. And I'm here to tell you, my man, once it dies it don't come back."

The song on the jukebox ended again, and only the faint voice of the bartender, who was now on the phone at the other end of the bar, filled the dead space.

"Give you a perfect example," Henry continued. "A couple years ago I'm watching this show on TV, right? One of them ones where people catch shit on tape, you know those? So in this one, they got this couple and they got this kid, just a baby, like one or something, in there. Still sitting in a highchair and can't talk and shit. Well both of them work so they hire this broad to watch their kid during the day, right? But after a couple weeks the kid's acting all weird. Kid was all happy and shit before they hired this broad and now the kid's crying all the time and acting all scared and shit, especially when they leave him with this broad. But the broad's all nice and lovey-dovey and shit with the kid when the parents are there, and supposedly she's got all these good references and all that, right? Well the parents, they decide to buy this camcorder and to set it up without this babysitter knowing, OK? So they do it and when they get home they play the tape and they see what's really been going on while they're at work every day. So on this show, they show this fucking tape, and let me tell you, my man, it's some of the most fucked up shit I've ever seen. This big fat broad spends the day hitting this poor kid in the head with wooden spoons and slapping him across the face—really fucked up beatings she's giving this kid—but she knows how to do it so it don't leave any marks, OK? And they show this shit right on the TV show, the kid's all screaming and crying and shit and this cunt's whacking him around. Defenseless, trusting, beautiful little kid." Henry stared down at the bar, his upper lip trembling with anger. "So I'm watching this and all I can think of is my own kids, right? I start remembering when they were that age, all little and helpless and shit, and how if anybody did that to them I'd fucking kill them. I'm watching this show and I'm seeing what this broad's doing and I want to just beat her fucking face. Now I ain't never hit a woman—that's pussy-ass shit, you ask me, no real man hits women—but this bitch, let me tell you, my man, I wanted to just hold her down with one hand and punch her fucking face out through the back of her head with the other one. And if I did, I should get a medal for it, far as I'm concerned, because any asshole that can do that to a little kid ain't worth a pinch of shit in a snowstorm in my book. They deserve to die. That *twat* deserved to die." He shook his head and seemed to remember I was sitting next to him, listening. "So anyways, they show the parents again

146

and they're all weepy and shit about how they can't believe it and how this broad betrayed their trust and all this. So they show this tape to the broad herself and she starts crying and saying she's sorry and all this, and you know what they do? They call the cops. The guy, this yuppie pussy, he calls the fucking cops. They show him when he's talking about what happened, and you can see in this guy's eyes, he wanted to kill the bitch. He needed to do something. And calling the cops ain't it. This bitch came into *his* house and attacked *his* kid. He needed to *do* something. You see what I'm saying? But he called the cops and they arrest the broad and you know what happened? A whole lot of nothing, that's what. This bitch gets put in some program for anger and abuse and all this shit, and she has to pay some fines and court costs and that's it. She don't do any time or nothing. So then they switch back to the parents, right? And this guy's talking about the injustice and all that, but you can see what's really going on in this guy. Even a yuppie wimp like him knows something inside him is dying. He knows he should've just dug a fucking hole in his backyard and killed the bitch, but he knows he didn't and he knows he never will. Heaven, Hell, the law, prison—there's a whole lot of things to be scared of, my man, but don't none of it matter if you can't live with yourself no more, am I right?" He paused long enough to take another drink. "We ain't so far outside those caves as we like to think, Andy, know what I mean? And you know what? That ain't such a bad thing. It's like in nature. Animals do it right.

One of them threatens the herd they take the motherfucker out. *Out.* They thin the fucking herd. No
bullshit about it, they don't make no big deal over it,
they just do it. Know why? Because it's what's got
to be done, it's the nature of things. And none of
them get in the way or tell them they're bad or what
they should or shouldn't do. No consequences. You
see what I mean? No consequences because it ain't
about should or shouldn't. It's about what's right
and what's got to be done sometimes. Hey, it's not
always pretty and neat and tidy, right? But what in
this world is?

"Take Dolores and Reggie, for instance," he continued a moment later. "I've been doing a lot of
reading. Never been a big book guy, but lately I've
been reading some books about the body — bones
and shit, mostly. And I got this crowbar. Heavy
bastard. I've had it for a while now. Keep it under
my bed. I tried talking myself out of it but I know it
just is what it is. I need to do what I need to do. It
ain't my fault my wife and my best friend decided to
fuck up my life and theirs. That's *their* fault, am I
right? So whatever happens, they brought it on
themselves the way I see it." He smiled, took
another swallow of vodka. The darkness in his eyes
had vanished, replaced by a disturbing sparkle.
"I'm going to take care of Dolores first. Then Reggie.
I was gonna whack them in their legs, right?
Figured that'd be best. But then I got to reading this
book, and I decided I'm gonna hit them right here."
He pointed to his upper chest. "Break their collar
bones. Very painful and a bitch to heal, that's what

the book says. So I figure I'll break their fucking collarbones. What are they gonna do to me, Andy? Put me in jail?" He laughed suddenly. "Probably. Do I care? No. Like I give a shit. Do I think it's right? Is it right to put me in jail for defending my fucking life, my sanity, my honor, my manhood? *Is* it? I don't know. I say no, but who the hell listens to me?"

"I'm listening to you," I said quietly.

He nodded then finished his drink. "You're a good man."

I looked down the bar. The bartender had been off the phone for a while and had resumed his conversation with the old man. I turned back to Henry. "I know you're in a lot of pain," I said carefully, "but don't throw your life away. It's not worth it."

Henry grinned like an amused child. "What is then? Tell me that. Anything? Anything worth it?"

Uncle's smiling eyes blinked through my mind. "I don't know, I—"

"You believe in fate, Andy?"

The way I felt at that moment I wasn't sure I believed in much of anything anymore.

Maybe that was the problem.

Before I could answer the door opened and a gust of freezing air shot through the bar. A man bundled in a coat, hat and gloves stood in the doorway with a scowl. He waved to the bartender, who then nodded and said to Henry, "Your cab's here, chief."

"Got to go, my man." Henry looked at me and shrugged helplessly, that silly drunken grin still plastered on his face attempting to hide what really lived there. He tossed some money on the bar, put a hand on my shoulder and gave it a squeeze. "Got a herd to tend to," he said with a wink.

The bartender came around the counter, helped Henry on with a long coat then walked him over to the cabbie. Once they had left he sauntered back to the bar, laughing lightly. "Don't worry about any of that," he said to me. "Henry's got problems." He pointed to his ear and made a circular motion in the air next to it.

The old man at the end of the bar let out a cackle of a laugh but said nothing.

"That stuff he told you about his wife and his best friend *did* happen," the bartender said. "But it was eight years ago. He broke down when it happened, lost his job and ended up on disability for his emotional problems. He lives in a room off of Main Street and comes in here every day, drinks himself silly and tells the same story to anybody who'll listen. Same one. Every day. I've heard it hundreds of times. When he's done and I figure he's had enough to drink I call him a cab and he goes back to his room and sleeps it off. The next day, rain or shine, snow or sleet, back he comes to do it all over again." The bartender cleaned up the mess Henry had left behind then wiped the counter down with his rag. "So, like I say, don't worry about it." He chuckled a bit harder. "But he gets you thinking, doesn't he? Crazy bastard."

"He's like the Devil," the old man said through crow-like laughter, pointing a crooked finger at me from the far end of the bar. "Don't listen to him, he just might have a point."

I forced a smile, hopped down off the stool and slipped into the phone booth in the corner. I flipped through the phonebook but there was no listing for the name I was searching for so I dropped a quarter in the phone and tried Information. The number came up as unlisted.

I hung up, returned to the bar and ordered one more drink. When the bartender put it in front of me I asked, "Do you know a guy named Joey Peluso, by any chance?"

He smiled. "I don't know anybody, OK, pal?"

"Local guy," I said. "Lives in town. You know him?"

"Who's asking?"

I dug out my wallet, paid for the drinks I'd ordered. I had a twenty and a fifty left. "Do you know him or not?"

He leaned close, forearms on the bar between us. "I know *of* him. Don't know him personally or anything."

"You know where he lives?" I dropped the twenty on the counter, slid it over to him.

"You know where South Street meets Covington Avenue?"

I did. I had grown up on South Street, and at the top of the road where it met Covington you could see our house and front lawn. "Yeah."

"OK, if you go straight you'll stay on South Street, so don't do that. What you want to do instead is turn left onto Covington. You follow that for about half a mile and you'll run into an old garage. *Ye Ole Yankee Body Work.* Joey Peluso's father owned it. It's closed up now, the old man died a couple months ago, but the sign's still up last time I went by. Anyway, Joey lives in the house, last I knew. Real piece of work, that one."

I nodded and he scooped up the twenty.

"Another drink?" he asked cheerfully.

But I was already on my way out the door.

* * *

Warden was no longer sleeping by the time I left Uncle's apartment that morning. It had come awake just as I'd once again begun to drown in my own thoughts and fears. I descended the steps, hopped on my bicycle and rode away with no idea where I was headed. Away. Just, away. The air was thick and my vision blurred, like a dreamscape covered in soupy fog roiling in off the ocean.

The next memory I have of that morning was finding myself standing before the small church we had attended as a family before my father left. Saint Anne's. The bike still balanced between my legs, I dropped the kickstand and climbed off, mesmerized by the face of the church: the large white doors, stained glass on either side, the beautifully manicured shrubbery leading to the entrance and the life-size porcelain-white statue of Mary holding the baby Jesus in her arms, gazing down on Him adoringly.

I walked slowly along the path to the entrance, unsure if it was all right for me to be there. We had stopped going to church regularly when I was still quite young, so my memories of this place were vague at best. And yet, I felt compelled to go inside and to see for myself what was really waiting there.

The doors opened into a small, narrow church with a high ceiling. The altar at the rear of the church was covered in a white cloth, and two tall candles in ornate copper holders were positioned on either side, in front. The windows that ran along the sidewalls were stained glass, multicolored faces of saints and saviors looking down upon me with reserved expressions and loving eyes. It smelled clean here, like someone had recently washed everything down with a heady cleaner of some kind, and I noticed how the wooden pews were polished to the point of reflecting what little light was seeping through the windows. To my left was the confessional box, dark curtains pulled closed over one side, a closed door covering the other. The light that signaled a priest was inside hearing someone's confession was off.

Stepping further into the aisle, I selected a pew, genuflected before the altar as I'd been taught as a child, and slipped onto the bench. It was cool against my legs and felt foreign, not like normal furniture but somehow more removed, less comfortable.

Behind the altar, on the back wall, an enormous crucifix hung, the dead figure of Christ hanging there, head ringed in thorns and face bathed in blood, hands and feet nailed to the cross, legs broken and the wound in his side evident even in dim light.

Boundless violence. Even here.

I looked away from the carnage to the pews ahead; saw memories of my father sitting nearby in his typical wrinkled suit, a younger version of myself next to him while the priest conducted Mass. My mother, also younger, happy and alive, sat next to him, Angela—just a toddler—in her arms. I tried to see my father's face but couldn't quite make it out.

"Why did Daddy leave?" I had once asked my mother.

She smiled through tears, touched the side of my face like she so often did and looked at me adoringly, like I had asked why the sky was blue. To her, it was a question as simplistic and naïve as that, and one she never answered.

Sitting in the silence of that church, I remembered my parents' bedroom and how it had been before my father left. For Angela and me it was a sacred place where we only dared venture if invited, and where we behaved differently than we did in the rest of the house. This was a place of mystery, unanswered questions and things that were forever just beyond our reach. It never looked quite as lived in as the other rooms in the house, like the bureaus and dressing table, the immaculately made bed and perfectly organized closets could have been display pieces in the front window of a furniture store. Lifeless furnishings that seemed posed, as if only there for the benefit of others who might happen to see them.

I remembered my father standing before a mirror

in that bedroom, the mirror over my mother's bureau because his did not have one. I remember him tying a skinny black tie and staring at himself in the mirror. I remember how haggard his face looked; the dark rings beneath his eyes, the shadow of his heavy beard and how evident it was even if he'd only shaved moments before. I remembered standing in the doorway watching him, wondering what he was thinking about and why he so seldom spoke to me. Even then I had no idea who this man was, or what he wanted. But I knew it wasn't me, it wasn't us. It wasn't *this*.

I missed him without knowing quite why.

Later, Ed Kelleher stood in front of that same bureau, arrogant and large and clumsy, rough and dirty hands grasping a small comb he used to perk up his brush-cut hair each morning, barking at my mother in his gruff and disagreeable voice, and when I would watch him from the doorway he'd react as if I were challenging him somehow, crossing into his territory, pissing on his turf like some vagrant alley cat come to fight for his tiny corner of the world. Only it wasn't his. It was mine. It was Angela's. It was my mother's. But that was something neither he nor I had fully understood until the day he returned from the hospital with a friend of his. He'd stayed in the car, slumped in the passenger seat, head looking down at the floor, dark sunglasses covering his eyes. I remembered his face that day, and the wooden crutches perched behind the front seat, poking out behind the headrest like errant bones. I remembered standing on the steps holding Angela's hand as his friend retrieved Ed's things from the house, and how my mother helped, bustling about awkwardly and trying to be busy rather than focused on the man outside in the car. A man too frightened to look at any of us anymore. A man broken by the same violence he used to try to break us, a man battered and bruised from being beaten and thrown down a flight of stairs, while somewhere, Uncle sat having a drink or smoking a cigarette, mingling with whoever it was he mingled with, smiling the smile of a conqueror, of an alpha male having protected the pack, and laughing as if all were right with the world.

Angela, still only five at the time, raised a hand to wave to him, but I caught her by the wrist and gently placed her hand back at her side. She looked up at me innocently. "It's OK," I told her. "Just don't wave goodbye."

"'Cause he spanked me?" she asked in a whisper.

I nodded; unable to take my eyes from the man slumped in that car.

Those visions faded, replaced by Angela, a bit older now, running through the woods behind our house, a look of terror and confusion on her tiny face, tears streaming and her mouth open as if torn by angry hands and set that way as she screamed silently in my mind. And from the shadows behind her, Michael Ring appeared, gaining on her, closer and closer…catching her…tackling her…dragging her down into the dirt.

Tears filled my eyes. "Where were you?" I asked the man on the cross.

Uncle beating Michael Ring mercilessly, bloodying him, executing him, butchering him in a sea of spraying blood and gore filled my senses.

"Are you here?"

I didn't realize until that moment that I had grabbed hold of the back of the pew in front of me, my grip so strong that my knuckles had turned white.

"Where *are* you?" My voice echoed through the open space, but it sounded like someone else.

And maybe it was.

14

It had gotten even colder, but it didn't faze me, my mind was a million miles away. I drove from the bar with three drinks under my belt and headed across town, toward South Street and Covington Avenue and Joey Peluso, the man who had murdered my uncle.

Louise spoke to me from the darkness. *"Peluso?...Are you out of your mind? You think you can show up on his doorstep and start asking questions like you're asking me? ...These kind of people, they'll kill you, understand?"*

I imagined what he looked like. Big. He'd be big. Muscular and wild-eyed, the kind of man you knew was dangerous the moment he walked into a room. A professional thief with a violent streak, not afraid to kill, maybe even the type who enjoyed it, got off on it, felt like a man when he was hurting and maiming other human beings.

The tire iron from my trunk was now on the seat next to me, ice cold and black and deadly, playing these games with me...

* * *

I pull up in front of the body shop. It's closed and dark, an old sign, pitted and dirty perched on the roof. I shut the engine off and then the head-lights. The car silently coasts closer. A single light on at the far end where the body shop gives way to the residential part of the building catches my attention.

Before I know it I'm out of the car, my feet crunching the rock hard snow as I cross the yard to the front door. Before I reach it a shadow moves by the window, peeks out at me. Joey Peluso is the kind of man you don't sneak up on. He's the kind of man who always sits in a restaurant or bar facing the door, so he can see who may or may not be coming. He's the kind of man who looks over his shoulder. He has his entire life, and will continue to do so until the day he dies. Until the night he dies. Tonight.

I hesitate when I see the shadow in the window, but when it moves away I continue to the door, the tire iron held down by my leg and covered by my long coat. With my free hand I give the door a few solid knocks.

"Who is it?" a deep voice asks from behind the door.

"Just passing through town," I say. "Had a little fender bender, wanted to get it fixed before I head out tomorrow. I saw your sign and—"

"We're closed."

"I'll pay top dollar, I really need this fixed. I've

got cash."

The locks disengage, as I knew they would, and the door opens slowly, cautiously. Peluso is as big as I imagined, more than six feet and over two hundred pounds. He wears a sweatshirt with no sleeves, a pair of jeans and boots. He's not a young man but his build is still powerful and sculpted. His arms are massive and covered in thick veins and a few tattoos. His hair is buzzed short, and he has not shaved in a few days. He looks me over without subtlety, then steps closer. "You deaf? We're out of business. Couldn't fix your car even if I wanted to."

His eyes are bloodshot and I can smell liquor on him. I wonder if he can also smell it on me, or if he can sense my fear or hear my heart thudding against my chest. I wonder if he looked this way the night he shot Uncle in the back of the head, spraying his brains out through the hole in his forehead all over the windshield. I wonder if he shot Uncle first or the other man — Ronnie Garrett. Were they laughing and talking when he shot them? Was Uncle afraid? Did he have time to feel pain or fear or was he simply alive one moment and dead the next?

"You sure you can't just take a look at it real quick?" I say stupidly, and I know this time he has sensed the tremble in my voice.

He glances beyond me, as if to be certain I'm alone then returns his attention to me. "You some kind of fucking retard, buddy? You hear a word I just said?"

I feel myself smile. The tire iron is so cold in my hand, like a dead frozen limb.

160

Peluso frowns, raises his head and subtly adjusts his stance. "Who are you?"

"Andrew," I say softly. "Andrew DeMarco."

As my last name registers, his frown deepens, and he steps forward, so close now I can feel his breath as it hits my face, hot and sour. "*DeMarco?*"

My mind screams at me, pleads with me to run, to turn and run and get as far away from all this as I can. But I stand as still as a man set in cement, eyes locked on his. "I'm Paulie's nephew."

He puts his hands on his hips and his suspicion slips away, replaced by what appears to be amusement. "*Paulie's* nephew? Didn't know he had one."

I nod, blink rapidly, sweating despite the cold.

"Real shame about your uncle," he says with a smirk. "We were tight a long time."

I say nothing.

"So you didn't come here about no car then." His eyes turn darker than before, black veils descending behind bloodshot whites. "What the fuck you want?"

I am barely cognizant of movement, like I've left my body for some other place, the car maybe, and am sitting there calmly and safely, watching the two of us in that doorway as in one fluid motion I pull my arm out from beneath my coat, swing the tire iron high over my head and smash it down onto the top of Joey Peluso's skull. I do it twice, with more speed than I thought I had. But Peluso doesn't move. He doesn't fall or try to avoid the blows or even make a sound. He simply stares at me, befuddled, like I've just told a joke he doesn't quite understand. We stand there locked in each other's stares for what seems forever, until I notice a small trickle of dark blood—so dark it's nearly black—glide slowly from his hairline down across his face.

It leaks slowly at first, like maple syrup, across his forehead, to the bridge of his nose, along the corners of his mouth and onto his chin. I watch as the blood gradually flows faster and stronger, and it is then that Peluso seems to notice it as well. But still, he doesn't move. He just stares at me for a moment longer, then without a word, he collapses, falls straight down to the floor like he'd been dropped from a platform overhead. His body makes a strange thudding sound as it collides with the floor.

I look down at him. His eyes are open, but they no longer see anything. His chest rises and falls every few seconds, but the intervals are longer each time. He is dying slowly, the blood from his head forming a growing puddle that fans out around him like a satanic halo. He makes a sudden wheezing noise, and his back arches, his legs shooting straight out as if he's been hit with an electric shock.

I notice the puddle of blood has nearly reached my feet. I step back a bit to avoid it, watch as it runs like a tiny river across the doorstep, chasing me into the snow and ice outside.

Peluso's body goes limp again, and I hear a hard gust of breath escape him in a gurgling rush. He lay still then, the flowing blood the only thing moving.

Leaned against my car, arms folded, a cigarette

dangling from his mouth, I see Uncle watching me. He has no discernable expression, neither acceptance nor disapproval. Nothing. Only a blank dead stare mixed with blood and brain sprinkled across his face, a stare that means everything…and nothing at all.

…I pulled over to the side of the road, my head spinning. The tire iron was still on the seat next to me. Stained neither with blood nor bits of skull, it was as clean and new as it had been when I'd removed it from the trunk only moments earlier. Parked on a side street near the neighborhood where I'd grown up, I drew several deep breaths until my dark fantasy faded.

I'd nearly gone through with it, was only a few blocks from Covington Avenue and the old body shop that surely resided there. Ignoring my shaking hands, I dropped the car into Drive and turned around.

I knew now where I needed to go.

Martha sits on the far edge of the bed, knees drawn close to her body, her chin resting atop them, arms hugging her shins. Motionless, contemplative, and swathed in shadow, she looks like a living sculpture, a fusion of supple flesh and deftly carved wood.

Her hair hangs forward, partially shielding her face Veronica Lake style, so that only one of her eyes is visible. At first glance she appears much younger than she actually is. The skin on her face is soft, taut and clear, and always has been. She claims the years of applying exotic moisturizers, creams and lotions are responsible, but I think it's simply a trait given her by higher powers, the way some receive striking violet eyes, gorgeous smiles or natural, effortless bodies that appear to have been sculpted from marble.

She scoops these creams from jars with her fingers, the way a bear cub scoops honey from a pot, then applies them with a tender efficiency I wish I could master in some way too, a natural poise and elegance that often leaves me feeling like an oaf stomping alongside a ballerina.

Although she is only a few feet from me, she seems impossibly far away.

I stepped from the car and moved cautiously across the street to the church. It had become so cold it was difficult to breathe, but I stood at the steps for a while just watching the doors and stained glass. I wasn't entirely sure why I was there, as I hadn't set foot in a church since the morning I'd sat in this same one all those years before, but I climbed the stairs and tried the door anyway, surprised to find it unlocked.

The interior was frozen in time, nothing out of place or changed since I'd last been there as a teenager.

As the door closed behind me I noticed a woman in a bandana near the altar. She had a rag in one hand and a spray bottle in the other, and though the church was nearly dark, I saw her smile at me.

"I'm sorry," I said, "is it all right for me to be here?"

"Of course." She gave a slow nod and motioned

to the pews. "I have to lock up when I'm finished, but I'll be here another half hour or so."

"Thank you."

As the woman resumed her cleaning duties I slid into the last pew, the one closest to the door, and watched the altar a while. The same enormous crucifix hung on the wall behind it, beauty and horror both. Life itself.

It's raining. I watch it sluice along the windows overlooking our backyard, slinking over the glass like a liquid serpent blurring the trees, the birdbath, the picnic table and forest beyond. It has been raining for days, but I don't mind. I love rain. I find it peaceful and cleansing, something that reminds me I'm alive on Earth.

Martha and I have spent the day inside, but later we'll go for a walk in the rain, and she'll tell me about her day, her voice barely audible over the thud of raindrops on her umbrella. Until then, we huddle indoors, quiet for a long while now, listening to our thoughts and the slow steady rhythm of the rain.

I turn from the window, watch her there on our bed, and when she notices my stare she raises her head slightly and blinks, awakened from daydreams. Her eyes drop from my face to the drink in my hand. "Why do you drink on quiet days like this?" she asks.

"To forget," I tell her. "Why do you?"

"To remember." She pats the bed next to her as if summoning a child or a dog. "Come here," she whispers.

And I do.

There is no quiet quite like the quiet of an empty church. I'd forgotten how profound that kind of silence could be, and opened myself to it, let it wash over me. Even with the woman wiping down nearby pews, I remained focused on the altar and the sculpture of Christ hanging behind it, remembering how when I was a child this had all seemed so real to me — alive and vibrant — sacred and holy. All these years later I had allowed God to become something impersonal and elusive, a phantasm obscured in distant mist, and while I still believed, it was in a manner far more mundane, the way I believed in the past, in the Civil War or The Great Depression, in a detached and analytical sense. The magic and mystery life once held had dulled elsewhere, so why not here too? Time had beaten them down, rendered them nearly useless.

"Nearly," I said softly, answering my thoughts, maybe my prayers. "But not quite."

I lie on my back; my head in Martha's lap, her hands and arms cradling me like an infant. I can feel the beat of her heart and the gentle caress of her warm breath as it pulses across my forehead and down along my neck. Her hair hangs over me like a curtain, and she smiles ever so slightly, eyes blinking slowly.

Rain sprays the windows as a delicate wind kicks up then vanishes as quickly as it arrived. Outside the world is clean and wet and trickling and dripping — alive and in motion — but here in our nest we are sheltered from all of it, near but apart, the advantage, or perhaps the price, of safety.

As her fingers stroke my cheek, I gently take her hand into mine; turn it over slowly to expose her palm and the scars along her wrist, carved there long ago when she was someone else. She allows me to study them, as I sometimes do, but I feel her tremble.

I look up at her beautiful face, at the scars that live there too, not embedded in her skin but hidden somewhere beneath it, and know she is also looking at mine.

I run my thumb across the scar tissue on her wrist, jagged like cracks in a desert floor. "I can protect you," I say.

"We can protect each other," she answers.

As Martha leans closer and we kiss, I feel the kittens stir at the foot of the bed, tiny paws reaching for us as they come awake. And as the rain continues to fall just beyond the walls surrounding us, we slip away to somewhere else. Together.

I wasn't sure how long I'd sat in the church, but it seemed quite a while. Though it wasn't terribly warm there, the chill I'd sustained outside had faded. As the cleaning woman slipped out of sight behind the curtain on the altar, I studied the scars of Christ, the crown of thorns and the blood forever engraved on His face.

"Did you know?" I asked. "Did you know what you were meant to become?"

I fought the emotion but it hit me in waves, one after the next, pulling me down like an undertow and holding me there. Memories came to me in mosaic, and I struggled to focus on them as they rushed through me: Henry in some dingy room over a pool hall, spending his nights drunk and clutching a crowbar like a lover, contemplating shattering collarbones with eyes glowing red like a demon. How easily he could be any of us. Boone alone in his apartment, staring at old photographs and thumbing through comic books, waiting for something—anything—to rescue him. Louise, in her vintage dresses and spike heels, smoking cigarettes, touching up her lipstick and sealed away in her glass booth, fighting to remember a brief moment of contentment and a life she never quite had, her lover's promise of happiness-ever-after always just beyond their reach. My mother, struggling with nightmares all too real, shuffling through the remainder of her life like an old car coasting on fumes, only vaguely aware of her life before, and the potential it held. Uncle, alive and dead and everything in between, slipping between memory and shadow, blood and laughter, smashing and destroying and loving and holding us, sitting in the front seat of a car before vaulting forward, the bullet smashing into him from behind and exploding out through the front of his head. His brains on the dash and windshield, his memories gone in an instant, his eyes turned to black, dead on a coroner's table. Gone. Martha at home with the kittens, waiting for me, part of her hoping I'd be back, another hoping someone else might walk through that door instead, someone changed, someone healed. Angela, young and innocent, older and wiser, both at once somehow, an angel soaring through flames then hovering just above them, wings singed but carrying her still with grace and strength. And amidst all of it—God and man—life and death, pain and joy exploded as one, drowning me in a dust devil of crimson tears.

There we sat, the man on the cross and I, as I wept like a child, uncontrollably and without reservation, my body bucking, eyes blurring, nose running and throat constricting, while everything gushed free of me like the blood that it was. For the first time in a very long while, I felt Him there with me, down from that cross, His hands in mine, murdered eyes alive and open, seeing me too.

I'm sure the woman heard my outburst, but thankfully she remained behind the curtains.

It wasn't until I heard the door open and felt the slap of cold air behind me that I even attempted to control myself. Wiping the tears away with the sleeve of my coat, I glanced quickly over my shoulder, certain I was caught in a dream.

Just inside the door, stood a woman partially hidden in shadow.

"*Angie*," I said, voice breaking.

15

She stood a few feet from the pew, unsure of what to make of me at that moment, I'm sure. Though it had been a few years since I'd seen her, bundled in a heavy black coat flecked with muted grays and whites, and a matching scarf and beret, she looked every bit the mature and confident woman she had become long ago. Still, I couldn't help but see the same little girl standing alongside her as well. Angela had gone on to become a successful prosecutor in Arizona, married with two children, but no matter how many law degrees she obtained or children of her own she had, to me, a part of her would always be the little sister who'd once followed me around like a loyal sidekick, the tiny waif on her bed surrounded by stuffed animals, storybooks and dreams.

She raised a gloved hand to a wisp of hair curling out from under the beret, the tip of which had come to rest in the corner of her mouth, and combed it away. "Are you all right?" she asked gently.

"Is this a religious vision or is it really you?" I laughed despite the tears in my eyes.

"It's really me, I'm afraid." Angela smiled, her bright teeth cutting the dim light, but I knew that her own tears were not far away. "Didn't expect to see you here."

I wiped my face clean as best I could and stood up. "Did you just get into town?"

"I landed at Logan about an hour ago, had a rental car waiting."

"Seen Mom yet?"

"No. I wanted to come here first." She stepped a bit further up the aisle, the heels of her boots clacking the floor as she looked around the old church, taking it in as if she'd never seen it before. "Just for a few minutes, anyway."

I stepped from the pew and opened my arms. She came to me like it had just then occurred to her to do so. I could smell her hairspray and a faint trace of perfume as we hugged, felt her heart beat against mine. She pulled away after a moment, fearful, I think, of lingering too long and allowing emotion to get the better of her.

"I called the local authorities this afternoon," she said quickly, assuming an official tone I imagined she used during press conferences. "Figured I'd get a little professional courtesy, but apparently they don't have many leads. They didn't seem terribly concerned about Uncle's murder, frankly."

"I know. Not too surprising, though."

"No," she said, her tone softening again. "I guess not."

171

"It's good to see you." I tried on a smile but it felt out of place. "How's Dean?"

"He's doing well."

"And the kids?"

"Great."

"How's Martha?" she countered.

"Fine, doing fine." I shuffled about, unsure of what to do with myself. "I'm sorry about before, I—"

"Andy, don't be absurd," she said through a sigh. "You don't have to apologize for breaking down at a time like this."

"Everything just sort of hit me at once, you know?"

She nodded. "I know the feeling."

"How are you holding up?"

"I've spent the better part of the day crying myself. I was so sure I had everything under control then it all just crashed down on me like a ton of bricks. It happens like that sometimes. I see it in court quite a bit, particularly when people are sentenced."

I could tell she was trying to focus on the subject matter in order to deflect emotion, and I went along with her, following her lead.

She moved away, a bit closer to the altar, and gazed at it reflectively. "Have you ever heard of Medjugorje?"

It seemed I had heard something about it on television years before. "Vaguely."

"It's a mountain village in Yugoslavia," she said. "Back in the 80s, six children allegedly encountered the Virgin Mary on a mountaintop there, and ever since she's visited them regularly in these religious visions that take them over. Supposedly, in these visions, Mary reveals several secrets to them about the future of mankind and the possible end of the world. The church hasn't confirmed it as genuine yet, even though apparently these apparitions are still taking place today. The young people having the visitations have undergone numerous medical tests, and it's been determined that there's nothing wrong with them physically or psychologically, and that they're not faking it, it's not a hoax. The jury's still out on whether what they're experiencing is supernatural or not, but they're definitely experiencing *something*. Anyway, it got so much press and news coverage that by the late 80s Medjugorje was known all over the world, and literally millions of people have gone there to see what it's all about, believers and nonbelievers alike.

"On this documentary about it," she continued, "they showed this horde of people who had traveled there from all over the world celebrating Mass one afternoon in the village, and all of sudden this one man left the group and wandered off on his own. He was an American, a middle-aged, everyday sort of guy. The camera followed him as he left the Mass and went off on his own to this small courtyard. He was obviously praying and trying to hold himself together, but then all of a sudden he just fell to his knees and burst into tears. His tears weren't the tears of an adult, though, more like a child. He knelt there wailing uncontrollably, totally broken and overwhelmed by what had to be some grand epiphany. One that tore him apart in some ways, but one that also set him free, guilt and shame, retribution and an awakening all at the same time. I'd never heard anyone cry like that before." She turned from the altar, faced me. "Until tonight. I've heard it twice tonight. Once from myself, and once from you."

"There's been so much pain," I said. "So much violence."

She nodded. "But there's also been joy."

"Both."

"Both," she agreed. "I don't know if what happened in some little Yugoslavian village on the other side of the world is real or not. Maybe it is, maybe it isn't. The point is, regardless of where we are or what happens or doesn't happen, we all carry what we have to carry in this life, we do what we do and we hope to God it's at least close to the right thing. I put people in prison every day of the week, Andy, and most days I know I'm doing good, making the world a better place, a safer place. Some part of me is putting Michael Ring away every time, part of me is putting Uncle away, putting them both to rest along with the little girl I used to be, each of us in our little boxes, like dolls no one wants to play with anymore. It's the only way I know how to do it, and for a long time it was the only way I could deal with it and still get through the day, you know?"

I'd never been prouder of my sister than at that moment. Success had been her revenge, success professionally, success as a wife and mother, as a daughter and a sister, as the decent and loving human being she'd always been. In the end, despite the pain we'd all felt, what took place had been perpetrated against *her*. The rest of us had been traumatized witnesses to the damage afflicted upon her, fellow soldiers wounded by the fallout of shrapnel from the grenade thrown into *her* lap. What had happened hadn't destroyed her then, hadn't broken her, and it never would. She was bigger, stronger and smarter than any of us, and had been from the start.

A few weeks after Ed Kelleher leaves, Uncle arrives at our house. It is early afternoon, a bright and sunny day. He appears with a plastic bag full of tiny tan rings that suspiciously resemble breakfast cereal. But when Angela and I ask why he is carrying around a bag of cereal he claims he purchased them from a mysterious man he'd met on a recent trip to New York City. "In a little shop, out of the way, on a dark little side street," he says gleefully. He tells us the rings are actually seeds, that when planted properly in fresh soil, yield a wide variety of doughnuts within hours.

Although I consider myself a savvy eight-year-old, he speaks about the power of these seeds with such conviction that it seems sinful to doubt him even for a moment.

"Do you believe?" he asks.

Angela's face breaks into a smile. "Are you teasing us, Uncle?"

"If you don't believe," he says, "they won't work."

"Then I believe," Angela says.

Uncle looks to me. "Andy?"

"Me too."

With our mother watching from the back door, the three of us clear a small patch of dirt in the backyard and begin planting the seeds. Once finished, Uncle announces he has a busy day planned and has to go, but promises to return later to see the results of our efforts. "Remember," he tells us, "you have to believe or the magic won't work."

As fate would have it, our mother suddenly remembers some chores she has to run. Angela and I object, but Uncle explains that it doesn't matter where we are once the seeds have been planted, just so long as we continue to believe as hard as we can.

The trip to the post office and local drug store is the longest fifteen minutes of our young lives. Each time I look over at Angela, strapped into her car seat like a dwarf astronaut, her eyes are shut and the words, "I believe," whisper from her lips again and again.

Apparently our collective faith is sufficient, because when we return home, jump from the car and bolt to the backyard, there in our garden are several varieties of fresh doughnuts protruding from the ground, impaled on objects that look an awful lot like tongue depressors, but that Uncle later verifies as "stems."

I laugh as Angela dances about, a doughnut in each hand and chocolate frosting from one side of her face to the other while lecturing our mother on the power of "believing really hard." My mother looks on, barely containing a smile, as Uncle dances about with Angela, having even more fun than the rest of us.

Of course it occurs to me that Uncle has simply pur-

chased a dozen doughnuts and displayed them in our absence, but it doesn't matter. It's more fun to believe.

It's more important to believe.

"I just spoke to him about two weeks ago on the phone," Angela said, bringing me back. She shook her head slightly and smiled, though her eyes had grown wet. "He seemed so happy. You know how Uncle was when he was happy."

"Like a little kid."

She laughed in agreement, but the tears spilled free despite her laughter, or maybe because of it. "I loved Uncle, Andy, and I always will. But he's dead now. He's out from under all the rest of it, and so are we."

I wanted to believe her, so I did. "You think Mom feels the same way?"

She smiled a quiet, sad little smile. "I hope so."

After a moment Angela strolled back down the aisle, put her arm around my shoulder and turned me toward the door. "Come on," she whispered. "Let's go home."

16

I parked in front of the house. The kitchen light was on, and I could see my mother hunched over the table with a drink in her hand, mourning the death of her brother while occupying rooms we'd once shared, a porter to ghosts in a realm long deserted.

I often dream of my mother in that house, older now and still paying for our sins, still smothered by the cocoon we'd all insisted upon and then abandoned her in. The dream is always the same. My mother is walking slowly down a dark corridor. The ceiling is low and the space between the walls narrow, the only light provided by a candle she holds in a pewter, ornate holder I have never before seen. When the dream begins I see her from quite a distance, at the far end of the corridor, moving closer, barefoot in an off-white nightgown that nearly reaches the floor. With each new step the hem swishes back and forth with a curious whispering that sounds as if she's shushing someone. She holds the candle high and out in front of her like a lost miner, coming closer still and eventually reaching a door at the end of the hallway.

The door opens with a creak. She steps into a modest room. There are windows there, through which traces of soft natural light emerge. I guess it to be early morning, perhaps that brief period of time just after dawn, when the world is suspended somewhere between total light and total darkness, a time when magic seems alive and well, when anything — even miracles — might be possible.

The room is bare but for a low, long table, at the end of which sit a porcelain basin and two stacks of neatly folded towels.

As my mother approaches the table, I see her more clearly. Her hair is drawn into a French twist that is gradually loosening and coming apart. The hair close to her scalp has turned a dull shade of silver, and the lines in her face are more defined, as if etched there by an artisan with a delicate sharp tool. Her eyes are tired, but thoughtful, *knowing*, in a way only a mother's eyes can be.

She places the candle on the table and looks down into the basin. A fat squishy sponge floats in the water. She reaches for it, pulls it free and wrings it out, the water trickling loudly into the basin.

It is then that I notice the water is a faint crimson, almost pink.

My mother washes her hands in the light cherry water, runs the sponge over her wrists and forearms — Lady Macbeth come to life, the blood in her visions diluted but alive — then returns the sponge to the basin and dries herself off with one of the towels. The towel is so white it seems out of place, but she takes no notice of this, simply dries herself with a slow efficiency and drops the towel in a heap to the table.

She goes next to one of the windows. There are three in a row along one wall. Narrow but tall windows with single panes of glass and frilly lace curtains hanging in each. Beyond them there is still faint light, but nothing else, emptiness within the light. She stands at the center window and gazes through it, at nothing.

From a series of wide cracks in the ceiling, snow begins to fall inside the room like elegant plump feathers. My mother smiles and raises her hands as if to catch them, tilts back her head and sticks out her tongue like a child.

And then I'm there too. Suddenly, and without explanation I am in the corner of the room. Sitting there, watching her. I am her child, her baby, and she is my mother, and yet, in this odd territory between reality and dreams, we're the same. Both blind mice reaching desperately through darkness for some sense of the divine and all the promises such a destination surely holds.

She moves through the snow to the corner, crouches before me. "Are you cold?"

"Yes," I tell her.

She crawls next to me and sits on the floor, back against the wall. "It's all right," she says, opening her arms.

I lean closer; allow her arms to encircle me, to draw me near. She is warm and soft and I feel safe there, where I began. I hug her back; hopeful my embrace makes her feel the same.

"You're all right," she whispers.

"But are you?"

She looks again to the windows, but never answers.

The snow begins to stick, to cling to us like a membrane. Slowly, the cocoon slithers over us, seals us off and holds us still. Even as it cuts off our oxygen, even as we struggle to breathe, even as the light through the windows fade and it all goes black, I can hear my mother's frantic, whispered prayers.

This time, rather than awakening in a twist of sweat-soaked sheets, I found myself sitting on the other side of the window, apart from my mother, but not for long.

Angela's rental car was parked ahead of mine in the driveway. She was sitting behind the wheel, there in the dark, waiting for me.

Hiding in my own patch of darkness, for some reason memories of Michael Ring's parents came to me. The only time I'd seen them was when they spoke out on a local television station not long after their son had vanished. I'd watched mesmerized and frightened all at once while his mother held up a photograph of her son, her eyes red and ringed with dark circles. She looked too old to be the boy's mother—maybe his grandmother—and seemed beaten down by any number of things, but mostly she seemed alone. Terribly, utterly alone. His father was a large man of few words, gruff and looking more embarrassed or put out than concerned. He too looked too old to be Michael Ring's father. None of it seemed to fit. Nothing seemed right.

And nothing was.

What did they do to you? I wondered. *And what have you done to them?*

What have you done to all of us?

My memories shifted to the day in Uncle's apartment, the day he gave me the truth I'd gone looking for. It was the last time I'd ever spoken to him, but he'd always been with me, and he always would be. Good and bad and everything in between, he'd always be a part of me, and me him. We were all together — *all* of us — forever, washing in basins of bloody water and trying to stay warm while snowflakes fell from cracked ceilings, blind mice all, suddenly able to see.

Michael Ring's disappearance remains an unsolved mystery to this day.

My eyes scanned the front yard. At first, all I saw was snow and ice glistening in the moonlight, but the darkness hanging over me no longer seemed quite real.

As the moonlight shifted I focused with such effort that just for a second I saw myself as a boy rolling around in the grass, giggling as Uncle tickled me.

"I can't stop until you say it!" he shouted playfully, hugging me close.

"Uncle!" the little boy laughed. "*Uncle!*"

Even now, I still hear that laughter from time to time.

I suspect I always will.

ABOUT THE AUTHOR

Greg F. Gifune's novels, stories and collections have been published in a wide range of magazines and anthologies all over the world, and have recently garnered interest from Hollywood. He is author of the short story collections *Heretics* and *Down To Sleep*, and the novels *Deep Night, The Bleeding Season, Saying Uncle, A View From the Lake, Night Work*, and *Drago Descending*. Also a freelance editor and Associate Editor at Delirium Books, Greg lives in Massachusetts with his wife Carol and a bevy of very cool kitties. He can be reached online through his official web site at: www.gregfgifune.com.

LaVergne, TN USA
04 December 2009
165962LV00004B/29/P